PITCHMAN'S BLUES

Jim Kelly

TEXAS REVIEW PRESS • HUNTSVILLE, TEXAS

Printed in the United States of America

This book is a work of fiction. Names, characters, places and/or incidences are products of the author's imagination or are used fictitiously. Any resemblance to actual events or locals or persons—living or dead—is entirely coincidental.

Requests for permission to acknowledge material from this work should be sent to:

Permissions
Texas Review Press
English Department
Sam Houston State University
Huntsville, TX 77341-2146

Library of Congress Cataloging-in-Publication Data
Names: Kelly, Jim, 1950- author.
Title: Pitchman's blues by Jim Kelly.
Description: First edition. | Hunstville, Texas : Texas Review Press, [2018] | Identifiers: LCCN 2018008616 (print) | LCCN 2018010291 (ebook) | ISBN 9781680031669 (ebook) | ISBN 9781680031676 (cloth) | ISBN 9781680031652 (pbk.) Subjects: LCSH: United States—Social life and customs—Fiction. | Short stories, American. | LCGFT: Short stories.
Classification: LCC PS3611.E44924 (ebook) | LCC PS3611.E44924 A6 2018 (print) | DDC 813/.6--dc23
LC record available at https://lccn.loc.gov/2018008616

Cover illustration courtesy of Anne Kelly, *Pitchman's Blues*, 2018
Cover design by Nancy Parsons

PITCHMAN'S BLUES

For Annie, my love and my muse

"I would unlearn the lingo of exasperation,
all the distortions of malice and hated"

Theodore Roethke

TABLE OF CONTENTS

Mountain Time

Scuffling For Coin

PITCHMAN'S BLUES

Pandora's Snap-Top Clutch

Great Aunt Alvena always kept a rusty blade straight razor close to hand, "just in case." Great Uncle Grover, her bachelor brother, knew things about ghosts. What made them mad. Why you should never look them in the eye. Things like that. They lived together in a second story walkup over the pool hall, beer parlor, lunch counter that Grover ran on the main street of El Reno, Oklahoma, my Old Man's hometown. We only met one time. I was six and they were both up in their eighties. This was before air conditioning. Heat smacks you in Oklahoma in summer. Smacks you from all sides. Makes you prickly and sleepy. They did not believe in fans, in using up perfectly good electricity just to move hot air around.

We drove from Michigan to Oklahoma in two days straight, my parents trading off driving and sleeping. Our car had dark vinyl seats, front and back. Frying vinyl when the fitted, terrycloth covers popped free. For pissing in a Coke bottle and not asking to stop all the time, I got a molded plastic cowboy hat as soon as we crossed the line into Oklahoma. By the time I figured out that the hat was a bribe it was already too late. My parents were off and gone. "Day or two," they said, disappearing into the dark at the top of the stair well. "We'll collect you in a day or two. Be a good boy, hear?"

Outside, when they left me, it was bright and hot, straight up twelve noon. Inside it might have been midnight. Against the heat, they'd nailed shut all their windows. Against the light, they'd covered them all up with long dark drapes. Thick drapes that humped up in folds on the floor. The only light that Great Aunt Alvena allowed in the front parlor came from three lamps, far apart. They smudged, but didn't seriously dent the dark of the room.

Claws. When my eyes adjusted I noticed claws. Every table, foot stool, floor lamp and chair had claws for feet. Big and little dragon claws. Some squeezed balls of polished dark wood, some of yellow tint glass.

Grover left soon after my parents to tend his business downstairs in the pool hall. "Don't stare," Alvena snapped now that we were all alone, "it ain't polite." Her face, inches from mine, was floating on black air. She'd slathered, layered her face and neck with a chalk white paste. It fissured with the heat, but mostly stayed in place. After she had the white laid down she got out her pot of rouge and "added a little color." Four bright red streaks started at her hairline on either side of her face. All eight, of varying widths, wandered down to the hollows of her cheeks, mashed up into something like circles there, then trailed off down to where her face quit and the dark picked back up.

"Long as you got color in your cheeks," she explained, "people know you're still alive and they let you be. I'm old and I take naps in chairs. My mouth hangs open. I look like I'm dead but I'm not. That's why I put the rouge on, so people know I'm alive. So they don't take a notion to haul me off and bury me when I'm only nappin'."

"I seen every last one of these," she said then, handing me a small basket with what looked like a jumble of oversized playing cards. "Seen them when I was touring Europe on my honeymoon." They were thick, antique postcards. Blurry photographs mounted on cardboard. Each one showed a similar scene: a wall, a doorway or shelf made out of human skulls. "How they stay like that and don't roll all over the place," she said, "is because they're balanced just right. Nested on bones. Neck bones, rib bones, hip bones, arm and leg bones."

She kept her straight razor in a black and red beaded, Bleeding-Heart-of-Jesus, snap-top clutch. The background was done in shiny black beads, the heart in shiny red. All the long, spiky top thorns poking into the top part of the heart were done in sun bright yellow. The scatter of fat bottom, tear shaped blood drops showering this way and that were, like the heart, done in a bright, fire engine red. Snapping open her straight razor, holding it up close so I could appreciate the rust pocked blade, she sawed a smile, a sort of half moon shape a few inches out from my throat. "Ain't much to you is there? Freckle face runt. Sorry little sack a bones. Kids tease you don't they? Beat you up for laughs. I know. I was puny too when I was your age."

"You know what the lockjaw is? It's when you bite down in this world and don't bite back up till you're in the next. It's a rust poison in the blood. Cut somebody good and deep with something nice and rusty, they'll get a dose and die. First thing happens, your teeth clamp shut. Ain't nothing anybody can do to make them unclamp. You can't eat, talk or swallow. Kills a full grown man in less than a day. Kill a runt like you in three, four hours."

Then we ate cookies, small hard cookies off a cracked, Custer's Last Stand China plate. It had seen better days. Mostly, the figures were faded down to silhouette, with more China white than battlefield blue showing. Custer was still upright and firing his pistol. The outlines of corpses were piled up around him with arrows, or parts of arrows, sticking up out of what was left of their backs and sides. A pair of skinny, white painted pipes rattled and clanged up the far wall of the cavernous, dark bedroom they left me in that night. I dreamed of slow motion straight razors inching my way. Of skull caves that went up and up forever. Of "the lockjaw" settling in, taking hold.

"Somebody hits you," Alvena advised over breakfast the next morning, "hit em right back. Hurt em good. Even if they beat you silly, hurt em and they'll think twice about ever starting something up with you again."

Great Uncle Grover wore saggy, bleached bib overalls. He rarely took his cap off, inside or out. It had two nickel sized wear marks on the bill where he always grabbed it. Once we were bouncing along a red dirt road in his rattly old pickup, he told me all about Geronimo's Ghost. How Geronimo had been a fierce warrior chief. How he still stood guard still over the battlefield we were headed for. "Kill us sure if he catches us taking anything," he said, "especially anything like arrowheads."

"If you do see him, run for your life. Run and don't look back.

Whatever you do, don't look him in the eye. Do that and you're a goner. He has the evil eye. He can freeze you in your tracks. Freeze you so you can't move, talk, shout for help, nothing. Then, when you're all froze up like a statue, he'll stroll over, easy as you please, and take his own sweet time cutting your throat."

Stopping abruptly in a swirl of red dirt, Grover got out and propped up the hood of his truck with a long stick. He was frowning down at the engine, all heat clicks, oil stink and steam. "Damn thing keeps cutting out on me at the worst times," he said. "I best stay here and study on it, see can I figure out why." Pointing off down a hill at a small mound of red dirt, he told me to look around and see if I could root out an arrowhead or two, but, to keep my wits about me. To stay on the lookout for Geronimo's Ghost.

That first mound had three arrowheads in it. Sharp point, scoop sided arrowheads. So did the next one, the next one and five or six after that. Down on all fours now, pockets full to bursting with arrowheads, I rounded a massive Osage Orange tree down at the bottom of the hill, down by a sluggish, muddy orange river. Moccasins. Suddenly, inches away, moccasins were all I could see. A pair of enormous, beaded and dirt crusted moccasins. Looking up I saw a towering wall of black and red, geometric patterned blanket. At the top, frowning down, staring me in the eye, was Geronimo's Ghost. Just like Grover said, he had a single feather, eagle feather, sticking up out of his headband.

Things move fast now, panic fast. Instantly, I'm standing next to Grover at the top of the hill. He's suddenly deaf and dumb. Doesn't understand a word I'm saying. Then, we're in the truck. He's trying, over and over, to get it started. No dice. I'm on the floor with my arms over my head, certain I'm going to get snatched or stabbed any next second. "Keep down," Grover shouts once the engine finally kicks in, stays running. "It's Geronimo's Ghost. He's coming our way, he's coming fast and he don't look happy."

Those two white pipes running up the bedroom wall whispered to me all night long. "Show us your throat, show us your throat, show us your throat." I knew I wouldn't live to see the morning.

Two days later, and staying with an aunt and uncle more my parents ages, I still could not sleep the night through. Every piece and patch of shadow hid a killer. Great Aunt Alvena with her straight razor. Geronimo's Ghost with a long sharp knife glinting in the dark. Same bad dreams over and over. I'm frozen stiff in a strange bed, in a strange, black dark room. I can't move or call out. I can't jump and run. I can't move a muscle. Slowly, out of the dark, moving my way . . .

"You got to get over this," my cousin Earl said after I woke him up a third time moaning and whining. "Like I told you, Crybaby, that old Indian you saw wasn't no more Geronimo's Ghost than I am. He's Grover's drinking buddy, Leonard Two Babies. He racks balls and sweeps up at the pool hall for beer money. Those arrowheads, Grover buys 'em by the sack full at the five and dime. Don't you know anything? Grover put your old man and my old man through the same shit back when they were kids. We've all been through it. Your old man wanted to make sure you got a dose of the same rotten stuff he got when he was your age. That's just how adults are. It's what they do. Get used to it."

He was sitting, now, on my chest, pinning my arms with his knees. "Listen up, Crybaby, and listen good. Don't wake me up again. You do and it won't be Geronimo's Ghost kills you. I'll do the job my own damn self. And I won't need no scalping knife or straight razor either. I'll kill you with my bare hands. You got that, Crybaby? Well, do you?"

Oklahoma Manners

Faces, and I know this for a fact, get rearranged nightly. My Old Man says so. Rearranged so bad sometimes that, come morning, your own sweet momma won't even recognize you. Makes you think, knowing something like that. Gives you ideas. Sometimes I wake up wondering if I've turned into a monster during the night. This happens to me all the time. I hold my fingertips an inch or so above my face, too scared to touch it and find out.

The last time I saw them all together, my eyes, ears, nose and mouth, forehead and chin, all right where they ought to be, they were in the bathroom mirror when I was brushing my teeth just before bed. But what about now? Middle of the night now?

They give me nightmares, but they're funny too, my Old Man's fight stories, his stories about rearranging faces. I have to hide in the dark to hear them. Hide under chairs and tables. Somewhere where he won't see me. Get caught and get my ass whipped. Whipped with his doubled over leather belt. He only tells them when he's drunk, drunk and drinking. Sitting up late with a buddy.

He isn't just a good shot, my Old Man, he's the best. Here's how I know. Every deer hunter wants to shoot a buck with big antlers. Every deer season, and always on opening morning, just at first light, my Old Man shoots a trophy buck. Never misses. Never takes more than a single shot either. Top that.

"I'm strictly a meat hunter," he says. "Coming up when I did, back during the Great Depression, the only meat on our table was what we shot. Momma cooked it all, squirrel, rabbit, duck, dove, mule deer, even possum sometimes. I do not hunt for fun, never have. I hunt to put meat on the table. I got no time for guys shoot more than one shot. If you can't kill it with a single shot, don't hunt. Stay home, learn to knit, play dominos with the old folks, but don't hunt. That's all I have to say on the matter."

When I grow up that's what I want to be, a meat hunter like my Old Man.

Our house is small and so is our kitchen. You can walk around a little bit over by the sink and stove. Pretty much the rest of the room is filled up with the picnic table. They really put on a show, my Old Man and his buddies, trying to get it in through our side door. Swore up a storm. It was great.

"Goddamn shame," my grandpa says every time he sees our picnic table. "Do you believe him when he says he bought it?"

"Don't let him hear you Dad," my mom whispers back, "you know how he gets. Please don't get him going."

"Stole it," my grandma says in her loud, I don't care if he hears me voice, "probably got drunk and stole it."

Galbait is my Old Man's best friend. They grew up together in Oklahoma. We see him once a year when he drives up to Michigan for whitetail deer season. "Once too often," my mom says, but not so my Old Man can hear. Years back, and before they were married, my mom took a train from Detroit to Oklahoma to meet my Old Man's parents. She got a surprise at the train station. Galbait, not my Old Man, was there to pick her up. He had to work a double shift or something. Anyway, he couldn't shake loose, so Galbait offered.

"The man was drunk," she tells it, "stumbling, falling down drunk and it was only eleven o'clock in the morning. Then, all the way from Oklahoma City to El Reno, he leans way out the driver's side window and shoots at things with a pistol. Road signs, jack rabbits, billboards, pop bottles in ditches, anything and everything. When he ran out of bullets he handed me the pistol, pointed to a half empty box of bullets on the seat and told me to reload for him, that he couldn't load and drive at the same time."

They got jumped, my Old Man and Galbait, in a bar in northern Michigan on the night before opening morning of deer season. Way my Old Man tells it, they were both dead tired and stopped as much for a break from the driving as anything. They'd been on the road for more than five hours and still had a good four to go to get to deer camp. "Last thing either one of us wanted was trouble," he says. "We just needed a chance to stretch our legs, eat a bite and relax a spell before we hit the road again."

I'm hiding when I hear this. Scrunched up back in under a dark piece of furniture in the next room. Still, I know what he's doing. I know exactly what he's doing. I can tell by the sounds. He's passing a bottle, sip for sip, back and forth across the picnic table with some loud talking buddy. "No need," he always says, "to dirty glasses or save the cap now is there? I don't social drink, I drink to get drunk.

"Place is packed see, smoky and loud. So smoky you can't hardly see half way across the room. Our food order's in and Galbait is easing his way back to our table, a drink in each hand. Then, he's gone. Disappeared. Some local joker tripped him. Another one shoved him hard in the back. He winds up flat on his face on the floor and everybody is laughing like crazy.

"I go to stand up and somebody cuts me. Cuts me all down my face with a broken bottle. See here, this little white scar all down my nose? Now look here, see how it hops all around down my cheek and chin, little bit of my neck?

"Now me and Galbait, we don't fight for sport, for the fun to it. We fight to hurt you. Hurt you quick and hurt you good so you can't hurt us back. It's how we were raised. Either one of us rearranges your face for you, it stays rearranged. Count on it.

"Shitty odds from the start. Ten to one, maybe more. And, like I said, it's smoky, so smoky, now I'm standing up, I can't hardly see. I decide to even the odds up and right quick. I grab a pool cue out of a guy's hand and start swinging. Teach these small town tough guys some Oklahoma manners. Now, I do not care how big or tough a man is, or how big and tough he thinks he is, you hit him in the face with a pool cue, fat side first, that man won't bother you no more. Guaranteed."

Sometimes when I mess with my Old Man, he pretends he's mad at me, really, really mad at me. "Keep it up little man," he says, cocking his fist like he's just about to let me have it, is just about to punch my lights out, "and we're gonna meet down at the hospital getting my fist pried out of your throat." He's a funny guy, my Old Man. Like at my last birthday party.

He'd been out all night and hadn't called. The party was started, me and my friends were eating lunch at the picnic table, my mom and my grandparents were in the living room talking. BANG. My Old Man ran our car into the front of the house. He didn't break through into the living room or anything, but he gave the bricks a good thump. Squashed a big old pricker bush, too. My mom ran down the hall crying and slammed the door to their bedroom. My grandparents said something loud out on the front porch, then my Old Man said something loud. Then my grandparents left.

Now he's standing in the doorway to the kitchen, and he's a mess. His hair is sticking out funny, his eyes are funny, his knuckles are all swoll up and his shirt is ripped. Ripped like somebody grabbed it up top and yanked it straight down, taking most of the buttons with it. He's blinking and shaking his head, like he's trying to get his eyes to work and they won't cooperate. Won't focus. That's when he falls on the picnic table.

What he falls on top of, starts right in snoring on, is this. My birthday cake. Two big bowls of chips. Eight paper plates with partly eaten hot dogs, pickles, and chips still on them. Eight paper cups with grape, orange, or cherry soda still in them. And the tablecloth my mom made special for the occasion. She dyed a sheet sky blue then painted birthday cakes with candles on them all around the edges in bright colors. Napkins to match. And those little crimp sided paper cups, the ones my Mom filled up with nuts and chocolate candies and put beside every plate at the table as a special treat for me and all my guests.

The Telegram

He always arrived unannounced and uninvited. He'd stay a day or two, never more than three. When he left he left early, before anybody was up and about. This was all after Great Aunt Iola died. After he sold their house in Elkhart, bought that secondhand camper, and hit the road. We lost track of him for years. Somebody said he stayed mostly in county parks that let you pay to camp by the week, but that he never stayed in any one campground for more than a month at a time. You never knew when he might come knocking.

Of course I'd heard about the telegram. It was famous in our family. So was Great Uncle Glen for sending it. Just walking into the telegraph office in downtown Elkhart one day, writing it out, start to finish, all by himself, then paying with his own money to send it. And him only ten or eleven at the time. But whose words were they? Did his parents put him up to it? Was the whole thing really his idea? Was he maybe just parroting what he heard his mom and dad say after they got the letter? Dot's letter asking for help? To this day none of us can say for certain.

I only saw it once, which was also the one and only time I ever met Great Uncle Glen face to face. He showed it to me himself. It was tissue thin and falling to pieces in his hands. Trouble is, he'd kept it folded up in his wallet for over seventy years. I was eight or nine and he was old, hunched over, musty smelling old. For most of his visit he stayed holed up on our screened-in back porch, painting. He traveled, those last few years of his life, with a two-page spread torn out of an old Life Magazine.

He kept it protected in a folder he'd made with two pieces of cardboard and a thick, masking tape hinge. It was a close up of Leonardo da Vinci's painting "The Last Supper." He used it as a template.

The glass he'd have cut to order at a hardware store. Painting supplies he bought at hobby shops. Thin handle, throw away brushes and little bottles of bright primary colors. Red, green, blue, yellow, the bold colors kids liked for painting flames all down the sides of model hot rods, shark teeth on the ends of spitfires, or squiggly, made up insignias on aircraft carriers and submarines. He'd center the two-page spread, set the piece of window glass on top, then get down to business. He was not, my Great Uncle Glen, much for detail. Close was always good enough for him. Pinkish swirl for a face, red, blue, or green smear for a tunic, dollop of dirt brown for loaf, chalice, or sandal.

When we woke that third day he was already gone. Propped, between the bread box and the toaster, as payment for his few days of room and board, was The Last Supper, or at least his bright and smeary approximation, on that cut to order piece of hardware store window glass.

I'd wandered too close the day before and surprised him. He grabbed me by the wrist and yanked me up close to his face. His breath was a stinky hot mix of coffee, licorice, and tobacco. He wore thick lens, yellow tint glasses. His eyes were two raisins. Gigantic, waterlogged raisins lolling in two split yolks. "Which one are you?" he demanded, twisting my arm hard and making me squeal. "Doesn't matter. You're all the same. Goddamn kids. Always snooping and spying. Never let an old man be. I suppose you want to see it don't you? You've heard the stories so you want to see it, right?"

His wallet was in the chest pocket of his bib overalls. It was a thick wad of a thing held together with wide, dirt dark rubber bands. It took him a long time to pry them all loose. It took him even longer to delicately sort through the mashed flat, stuck together contents.

When Glen was a kid his only sister, Dot, ran off with a married man. Cornet player for John Philip Sousa's marching band. Not only was he married, he had three kids. They hopped a late night train out of Elkhart for St. Louis. That's where they set up housekeeping, St. Louis, Missouri. Things went south pretty quick for my Great Aunt Dot and the coronet player. Soon after they got to St. Louis he went to see a doctor about a sore on his upper lip that wouldn't heal. It bothered him when he was playing. The doctor told him it was cancer. He could have it removed, quit playing the cornet, and maybe live out a normal span of years. Or he could play and take his chances. He kept playing. Six months later he was dead. Dot wrote to her parents for help. Asked for money to bury the cornet player and for a train ticket home. That's when Glen sent the famous telegram.

Years later I met my Great Aunt Dot. She was running a junk shop out of her home. She lived in a little house on a dirt road just south of Elkhart. How she got back from St. Louis and where she got the money to set herself up in the junk business nobody knows. We were taking a family car trip and stopped by late morning for a visit. Dot kept cats. Had more cats than I could count. They were everywhere in her shop. Asleep on shelves, sneaking under tables, lounging in boxes of two-for-a-nickel pillow cases, everywhere. As a little kid Dot was cleaning a rabbit her dad shot, cut her hand, caught some blood disease, and never again had a working sense of smell. Lucky accident. Open the door to her shop too fast and the stink of cat piss hit you full in the face. Made you blink, cough, and gulp for air.

But if the air was ripe in Great Aunt Dot's junk shop, the light was lovely. Was magic. She had shelves built across all her windows. Layers of shelves. Bang up next to one another, all along those shelves, were bottles of all shapes and sizes filled brim full with colored water. Every bit of light entering her shop got changed, made better. Turned red, blue, yellow, or green. Move your hand, your arm in any direction and it changed color. Pick anything up, move it around and the same thing happened.

A big woman, Great Aunt Dot hugged me up off my feet. She kissed the top of my head and told me a secret. When she took my parents in the kitchen for coffee I was supposed to stay behind in the shop. I could have any one thing I wanted. There were two conditions. It had to be something I really, really wanted and I couldn't tell my parents. It would be our secret.

"You're much too young for a pocket knife of your own," my Old Man said anytime I asked for one. "Too young and too clumsy." Propped, on a wedge of Styrofoam in a glass case, was a pocket knife. By my lights, it was perfection itself. It had a wolf howling at a big moon on one side, a gigantic bear crashing through bushes on the other. It had two good blades that snapped out, then snapped back in with a delightful click. There was no rust on either of them. I was holding it in my hand, transfixed, when Dot sneaked back into the shop. "Is that it?" she asked in a whisper. "The one thing in my shop that you absolutely cannot live without?" Speechless, I nodded yes. "Okay then. Hide it down deep in your pants pocket. And make it quick. We don't want that hothead Daddy of yours finding out and making you put it back."

When Glen spoke his voice was scratchy and hard for me to understand. But when he read it got clear, each word strong and separate. "Bad comes to bad." He paused, looked me in the eye, stared until I looked down, looked away. Then, holding the tissue thin telegram up to his thick lens, yellow tint glasses again, he continued. "You have sinned. You have shamed your family. You are dead to us. Same as if you was buried in the ground. You have made your whore's bed, now lie in it. Please make no further contact. Your Family."

Maude's Migrations

Oldest woman on earth when she finally died. What was she, a hundred and twenty? Old anyway. Older than old. Yes, that Lizzie. Lizzie the snitch. Lizzie the scold. You're right, she never once gave any of us a smile, a hug or a word of encouragement. Never a present, not even a card for birthdays or Christmas. Nasty right up to the end. Put a curse on anybody who'd sit and listen. Still, she had her reasons.

Listen. Here's what I heard. Things about Lizzie. Things we never knew growing up. Things they didn't tell us back when she was still alive. Did you know that she was orphaned at nine? That she lived with strangers after that because she had no family left alive to care for her? Worked, according to Aunt Ruby, for next to nothing. For food, shelter and cast off clothes. Did you know that she never even made it through third grade in school?

At sixteen she was married off to a man near seventy. Sixteen! That's what Aunt Ruby says. Guy was a retired railroad engineer. Long term lodger in the boarding house where Lizzie worked. Lived and worked. He was quiet, quiet and shy. So, he paid the landlady to make his case to Lizzie. Wanting to keep her ten dollar fee, which was a lot back then, the landlady made things simple. "Marry him or get out."

Two years after the wedding, and no more than six months after the birth of their only child, Otto, our Grandpa Otto, Lizzie's husband went simple. Just like that. Here one day, out to lunch the next. Aunt Betty is the one told me that. Said for the last four years of his life he sat in a chair by the radiator, a quilt over his lap, napping, staring off and giggling to himself.

His estate? He left her six pairs of bib overalls, a monthly pension of forty dollars, and his potato watch. Remember it? Big lump of a thing she kept on the table by her bed? Railroad slang because of its size, its heft. That's what Uncle Slick said. Said it was a piece of junk too. Wasn't worth more than three bucks, even on a good day. Uncle Glen said it was accurate as hell, never losing more than a second or two a year. Anyway, she never did sell it.

After the funeral they stayed on in the boarding house, Lizzie and Otto. They got moved to a smaller room. A room off the kitchen. That's where Lizzie worked, cooking, serving meals, then cleaning up after. Nobody taught her, but she was good with needle and thread. Just took to it. She started taking in piece work, doing alterations. Ripped out and rebuilt overcoats. Let things out and took them in. Suits and dresses, pants and skirts. She'd make new if you wanted, worked from scratch or a pattern, your choice. She was that good.

Remember hearing that she used to work at Lundquist's Department Store? Well, it's true. She got work as an assistant to the head tailor. Then, a few years later when his eyes gave out, she took over. Worked there the whole time Grandpa Otto was growing up. According to Aunt Ruby, every extra cent Lizzie ever made went to Otto. Her Otto. New clothes for school. New shoes and coats. Warm hats and mittens for winter. And piano lessons. She insisted that he take piano lessons.

This next part you already know. About how he was tall for his age and got full time work when he was only sixteen playing piano in the silent movie houses around Gary and Hammond. Remember he told us that to get the job he had to show he had his own sheet music? Sheet music for anything that might be going on up on the screen? Chase music, storm music, fight music. Remember that he could play it all, fifty-some years later, from memory, mixing in boogie-woogie here and there just to make us laugh?

And it was in World War I that he got his leg blown off. He was over in France in the trenches. He never talked about it to us, but that's what happened. They said he came home with a government issue wooden leg and a head for numbers. Set up a business with two guys he'd served with, been shot up and done rehab with. The same business he had when he died. They built it up, those three, out of nothing.

Once Otto starts making good money, steady money, money enough to support the two of them, Lizzie quits her job at Lundquists's. Quits it cold. Tells him, "Otto, I've always supported you. Now, it's your turn to support me." She never again worked outside the home. Free then to stay up late, sleep in, Aunt Ruby says Lizzie started in listening to baseball games on the radio. Night games. Games in far away cities. Cleveland and New York, St. Louis and Kansas City. She'd keep box scores for her favorite teams. Keep them in spiral top notebooks. One notebook for each team she followed. But, she never once went to see a live game. Never watched a game on TV. Voices in the night, that's what she liked. Voices late at night from far away cities telling of wild pitches, dropped fly balls, bases loaded, inning ending strikeouts. Blown chances.

Did you know that on the day Grandpa Otto and Grandma Maude got married Lizzie moved in with them? That very day! And, for the next twenty three years, in rented rooms, apartments, and later in houses, she never left. Not for a week or two. Not for a day or two. Not ever. Did you know that? I didn't.

You know how she was. All the time telling everybody how to do things. Set the table, peel an apple, sit in a chair. When to talk, when to shut up and how to eat your food. That's what it was like for Grandma Maude from day one of her marriage. Nothing she could do right. And nothing was ever good enough for Lizzie's Otto.

That summer they built the cottage. That's the summer Grandma Maude finally put her foot down. Told Grandpa Otto she'd had enough. That she wouldn't live under the same roof with Lizzie for one minute more. Anyway, that's how Grandma Maude's migrations, and ours with her, began. Remember, as soon as we got out of school for summer vacation we'd all go up north to the cottage with Grandma Maude? All the kids and the moms? Remember how Grandpa Otto and the dads used to drive up late on Friday nights, then drive back down Sunday nights for another week of work in the city?

What they never told us were the terms. Lizzie got to stay in the house in Detroit with Grandpa Otto, her Otto, all summer. But, she could not come to the cottage. She was banned for life from ever coming to the cottage. That's why we never saw her there. And, when we all came back south in the fall for school, Lizzie had to be gone. Out of the house gone. Out of the state gone. St. Petersburg, Florida gone. So once the terms were set and the migrations up and running, Maude and Lizzie never saw each other again. Not ever. Think about it; Lizzie out lived Grandma Maude by twenty-two years and Grandpa Otto by twenty-four. So my question is this: why, when there was no longer any reason for the ban, did nobody in the family ever invite Lizzie north? Let her stay at the cottage for even one single night? Knowing what they did? Knowing how it was for her coming up? What all she went through?

"Because she was a bitch, that's why."

Funny, that's exactly what Uncle Slick said when I asked him the same question. Hey, wasn't it Slick she left the box of corsets to in her will? Box of corsets and three dead geraniums? Wasn't that Slick? I thought so.

Our Secret

Rules, rules and more rules. Do this. Don't do that. World is trouble. World is danger. World will kill you if you don't watch out. Want to stay in one piece? Obey the rules. Break a rule, any rule, who knows? Who can say? Maybe we find your body, maybe we don't. You hear me? You hear what I'm saying to you? Poison builds up, little by little. Builds up and never goes away. Get one too many bee stings and you're dead. Same thing with wasp stings, hornet stings, spider bites. Anything with teeth can kill you. Skunk, possum, fox, any rabid anything. Dangerous stranger offers you candy out of a bag, you get in his car, we'll never see you alive again. With all of this, the lake was still the biggest taboo, drowning the biggest fear.

Don't swim after eating. Wait at least one full hour. Swim too soon and you'll sink like a stone. Sink and never come up. Cramp, sink and drown. Not a thing in the world we can do about it. Don't go down to the lake alone. Always have an adult present. Always, always, always. We can't prevent what we can't see. Say you sneak off and go for a swim, get out deep and get into trouble, what then? You'll drown, that's what. You'll be dead and gone before we even think to miss you. Miss you or go looking. You want that to happen? Well do you?

Our side of the lake was shallow at the shore and stayed shallow way out. You'd really have to work at it to drown on our side of the lake. You had to walk and walk and walk before it even got half way up your chest or anywhere near your neck. It got deep, but slowly, gradually, a little bit at a time. Nothing sudden. No drop offs. No sink holes. No real danger. Now the other side of the lake, that was a different story. There it got deep quick, over your head deep. Deep, rocky, and rough.

Awake early, pitch black early, on a summer morning. I put on my bathing suit and snuck out. Thick mist everywhere. Steaming up off the sandy path, out of the dark pine boughs and up off the boathouse roof. The painted board steps down to the lake were dew, slick and chilly on my feet. Half way down and I was invisible, hidden from the cottage windows by the dark and the slope of the hill. Not looking right, left, or over my shoulder I walked straight out into the lake, stopping when the water got waist high. Mist swirls were standing up all around me. Across the lake the dark outlines of trees, light behind them beginning to widen and seep. Shapes coming clear. Colors and shapes. Boats, rafts, shoreline and docks. A sunk, bright, plastic bucket.

"It's not nice," someone is saying close by, almost in a whisper, "sneaking up on a body like that." Behind me, in the dark, on our little square of cement outside the boathouse door, was Grandma Maude in her housecoat, sitting on a lawn chair and smiling, looking my way. Putting a finger to her lips for quiet, she waves me to join her. Wrapping me in a towel, she hugs me up onto her lap, then swears me to secrecy. Her special friend, she explains, is set to arrive any second now. Nobody knows about him, not even Grandpa Otto. We had to be quiet and still. Completely still and absolutely quiet. Any sound, any movement might scare him off.

Hose neck bobbing and a long sharp beak. Stick legs and skinny, three toed feet coming clean up out of the water with each slow step. Stops, freezes in place. WHAP. Spears a small fish, tilts it to the sky, swallows it whole. Walks right up to our dock, stops, sinks down, squat-walks underneath, rises on the far side, reassembles, then disappears off into the mist.

"Our secret," Grandma Maude says, giving my shoulders a squeeze. "You don't tell anybody about my special friend and I won't tell anybody that you came down to the lake alone. Deal?"

Asking Oscar

Ivory white, pearl white, soap white, skinny and tall, one-legged, hopping fast. BANGSLAP. Then again. Again and again. Louder and closer. Terrified, staring at the monster filled hallway outside the open bunk room door. The hallway was narrow with thin, pine board walls and a hard, concrete floor. Chalk white blur, he made his final hop, grabbed the sink, hit the light switch and slammed the bathroom door. Grandpa Otto, I discovered that morning, slept naked. Slept naked, except for a ribbed, cotton stump sock. The one bathroom in the cottage was directly across from the bunk room door. He traveled there for his morning wash up in the dark, bang slapping those thin board walls for balance between long, one-legged hops.

Saturday mornings he made a "work detail" for my Old Man, my Uncle Slick, and any other man staying the weekend. His place, his rules. He had them building dock sections, cutting down trees, clearing brush, digging flower gardens for Grandma Maude, painting, anything that needed doing. Once they were up and at it, he'd tilt back in his easy chair out on the screened-in front porch and relax. He got boxes of cigars from Cuba through the mail and smoked them, one after another, all day long. Mostly staying in his easy chair, he read murder mysteries, joked with us kids, took naps and told stories with his pals who were always wandering by. He did no work around the cottage himself. That was just understood.

If we got lucky, and always just before bed on a Saturday night, he'd call one of us over to do the secret knock on his wooden leg. That let

Oscar know we'd done all our chores and wanted to ask him a few questions. Oscar was the white mouse that lived in Grandpa Otto's wooden leg. We had to be certified ready for bed, teeth brushed, bunk room clean, all toys put away. We sat lined up on the bamboo, sun bleached old couch across the room facing Grandpa Otto. Always, he was in shadow in his tilt back easy chair. The only light on the porch after sundown came from two candles on round metal holders bolted to the wall just above our heads. Ragged bits of orange light flared and shifted with each puff of wind through the big, bowed-out screens that went all round the porch. Nothing was clear, solid, or still.

We could only ask Oscar one question at a time, and then only when it was our turn. No getting off the couch, no coming over and trying to see Oscar up close, and no petting. Once Oscar started to yawn, that was it. If you didn't get your question in you'd have to wait until next Saturday night. But, Grandpa Otto always guaranteed, you'd be first up next time. Mostly we asked silly questions so Oscar wouldn't get tired too soon. Would it rain tomorrow like Uncle Slick said? Would we catch enough yellow belly perch for a fish fry dinner? Things like that. Once, though, I had a tough question for Oscar. It was a question we all wanted answered.

Wading along the shore that morning with Grandma Maude, picking wild blueberries off the bank into little tin buckets, we found a pile of bones in the shallow water. Fuzzy-edged, green brown bones. Hip, leg and rib bones. Big bones. No skull but we knew, from the second we saw them, they were dinosaur bones. Grandma Maude agreed. From the looks of them, she said, they were certainly dinosaur bones. Very rare. Probably valuable. But, we had work to do. Until we finished picking enough berries for two pies we had to let the bones be.

My Old Man, Uncle Slick and Bill Brown, a local handyman, were taking a cigarette break when we showed up with the bones in our arms. They were in the boathouse talking when we arranged the bones, one by one, all down the dock to dry in the sun. "Goddammit," Uncle Slick shouted, "get those stinking deer bones off my fresh painted dock. NOW. Get 'em off and wash that filth off pronto, or I'll kick your sorry little asses from here to town and back."

We explained that these were not deer bones, but dinosaur bones, rare and valuable dinosaur bones. Probably worth a fortune. "What you found," my Old Man said, "is what's left of a jacklighted deer after old Eno gets through butchering it to feed his family. He dumps the evidence down at the far end of the lake, just where the swamp starts, so he won't get caught and hauled off to jail by the DNR."

"Idiots," Bill Brown said, cackling his rattly smokers' cough laugh at us.

"Morons," Uncle Slick said, spitting for emphasis.

That night I told Oscar the whole story, start to finish. Told him what Grandma Maude had said and what the men said. Oscar was sitting on Grandpa Otto's knee, facing the couch. He nodded when I finished up, then nodded for Grandpa Otto to lean down and hear what he had to say. When Grandpa Otto sat back up, Oscar was gone. He'd disappeared, just like he always did when he got too tired to take any more questions. Quiet for a minute, Grandpa Otto eventually leaned forward, his face out now in the flickering candle light. "Oscar says that what you found are definitely dinosaur bones. Genuine, museum grade dinosaur bones. Probably from a Tyrannosaurus Rex. And, he wanted me to tell you that your fathers, your fathers and that simpleton Bill Brown, wouldn't know a dinosaur bone if it snuck up and bit them on the ass."

Model Behavior

Every kit model had an action painting on the boxtop. That's what stopped us, froze us in our tracks. They were lined up on shelves at the front of the town's one drugstore, boxtops facing out. Swivel turret tanks blasting buildings down to smoke and rubble, hot rods spraying gravel, up on two wheels, fighter jets banking hard, spitting fire. My favorite was a De Havilland, a World War I bi-wing. It was an open cockpit fighter plane. The pilot was wearing a leather helmet and goggles. A long, white scarf blew straight out behind him. As he soared up into the blue sky a flaming German Fokker was nose diving in the distance. I was that pilot.

We hardly knew Cousin Phil when he showed up that summer. He was staying with us at the cottage because his mom, my Aunt Connie, was sick in bed and couldn't take care of him. Because his dad, my Uncle Chuck, was nowhere to be found. I can't blame them. I'd fake sick or disappear, too, if I had a kid like Phil. Still, he was a wizard at building kit models. Hands down, he was the absolute best we ever saw. Wood, metal or plastic, hot rod, fighter jet or battleship, it was all one to Cousin Phil. He'd trim and shape every last piece so they fit together just right. No glue bumps or gaps. And paint? He did it all free hand. Never once used a decal, he was that good. Spike tipped flames roared down the sides of any hot rod he built. Crazy big, sun yellow tiger fangs dripped blood from snout tip to cockpit of sleek, World War II fighter jets.

It was half way through summer vacation before I had enough money to buy that kit model of the De Havilland. Back at the cottage I set up our ancient, fold leg card table on the front porch, spread it with newspapers, slit the cellophane and opened the box. Horrified, I stared down at the contents. Spines. Stacks and stacks of brittle, gray plastic spines with tiny, ooze sided pieces branching out. Mad for the images on the boxtops, I'd never bought or built a model myself. Where, in that nonsense tangle of gray drab plastic, was my dogfight dream? Cousin Phil pulled up a chair, smiled and made me an offer. He would build it for me. Would make me the best De Havilland anyone had ever seen, Uncle Sam Top Hat insignias on both sides, wheels that turned, crisscross wires between the wings, twin mount machine guns up front, the whole deal. There would, however, be certain conditions. Rules I'd have to agree to. Once the De Havilland was finished, was mounted on the curved plastic base, banking, forever and a day, up into the lethal, dogfight blue sky, it would belong, temporarily, to Phil. Full ownership would transfer back to me at an unspecified future date of Phil's choosing. In the meantime, I had to do whatever he told me to do, "promptly and without question." Failure to comply, any failure, and the deal was off. The deal was off and the De Havilland was Phil's to keep. His property, free and clear, from that day forth.

And so began the tyranny of Cousin Phil. A snap of the fingers, day or night, got me up and running. Terms being terms, I could question nothing. "Move it or lose it," he'd snarl if I ever hesitated for more than a split second. Slapped awake at midnight, I was ordered to bring him two medium-thick slices of Velveeta cheese, precisely one half glass of ice cold milk, no more, no less, and eighteen M&Ms within two minutes. Once, with my Old Man standing just outside the front door to the cottage, Phil ordered me to sneak into my parents' bedroom, get two cigarettes from my Old Man's pack of Camels, get a fresh pack of matches out of the junk drawer in the kitchen, a pack with no matches missing, not a single one, and deliver the goods in under a minute.

At some point I began to balk. To pause. To not just instantly, slavishly run off in a mad frenzy. That's when Phil changed his tactics. Sweetened his tone. Smiling, he'd put an arm round my shoulders and say, "Little Cousin, I was going to give you the De Havilland today, but now . . . " And, for awhile, that worked. Got me up and running, off and gone at his every finger snap. Until, that is, the last time. Phil, stretched out on the end of the dock, gave me a command without opening his eyes. It was eleven in the morning. After eleven all snacks were banned, forbidden, it being too close to lunch. He gave me two minutes and thirty seven seconds to return with one thinly sliced, lightly salted piece of turkey from last night's dinner, a bowl with twenty six potato chips in it, none cracked or split, a glass of Coke with three ice cubes, full cubes, no partials, and, in a separate bowl, twelve dry roasted peanuts from Grandpa Otto's private jar, the one he kept in the cupboard up over the refrigerator with the liquor.

Halfway up the stairs to the cottage I stopped, turned and looked back down at Cousin Phil. He was never going to give me the De Havilland. I was always going to be his slave. Understanding this, suddenly, completely, I took off running. Betrayal, like electricity, must travel through the air. Exactly when I started running, Phil did too.

I slammed and locked the front porch door behind me, then slammed and locked the bunk room door. Hard soled, thick heeled cowboy boots quickly on, I grabbed the De Havilland, smashed it on the concrete floor, then stomped it flat. When he got in it was too late. The De Havilland, that beautiful, flawlessly built De Havilland, was a scatter of tiny, unrecognizable bits of busted up plastic. Screaming and spitting, Phil punched me hard in the face, over and over. Dancing, ducking, bleeding and crying, laughing, I shouted back, "I was going to give you the De Havilland today Cousin Phil... BUT I decided to dance on it instead."

Snakes

Water snake bites you, it won't let go. Not ever. I know. One bit my little cousin on the wrist. She was just sitting in the shallow water minding her own business. Then she's screaming and screaming, a fat black water snake clamped on tight. Shake her arm hard as she could, that snake would not let go. Uncle Leo snatched her up out of the water, Uncle Slick held her down on the beach, held her arm still while Bill Brown the, handyman, beat that snake with a long handled shovel. Mashed flat, stone dead, pulp and nothing but, that water snake still would not let go.

Snakes were everywhere, were all over the place at the cottage in summer. Skinny, quick, green snakes in the tall grass and flowers out front. Fat, gray, slow motion snakes slithering in and out of holes by the wood pile. Did they really swallow chipmunks whole like Cousin Phil said? Water snakes though, water snakes were the worst. Water snakes terrified me. They lived all along the lake shore in rock piles. On hot days they would coil up like hoses, blue black, black brown, yellow green, fish stinky hoses and sleep for hours on rocks in the sun. They swam lightning fast. Sometimes they swam with their heads up so you could see them coming, sometimes not. That was the worst part, never knowing where they might be and imagining them everywhere, invisible and tearing around under water, ready, any next second, to sink their fangs into your back, belly, feet, face, or sides.

A few days before all this happened the men set up Grandpa Otto's enormous old army surplus tent out behind the cottage for us. It had mesh windows, a fold back flap for a front door, and stunk of mildew and rot. Our sleeping bags, zipped shut to keep spiders out, were lined up in two rows across the tent floor. The plan was for all the kids to spend the night in that tent. Why, once it was up, didn't we? Collective cowardice. Afraid of the dark, but not wanting to admit it, we kept offering up that the tent needed a few days more to air out, to stop stinking so. "How about tonight," the men kept asking, chuckling, shaking their heads in amusement when we said not yet, maybe tomorrow.

On the day this happened I was down at the lake trying to catch minnows in a small tin bucket. Berry bucket. I was sitting still, not moving a muscle, the bucket on its side under water. Tiny minnows surrounded me, nibbling my back and sides, my toes. If I didn't move, if I let them keep nibbling, my logic ran, they'd get comfortable, get careless and swim into the bucket. "Snake!" somebody yelled. "Snake coming your way." I knew it was a lie. One of us, on dry land, was always yelling at any of us who might be out in the water. Bad joke, but it usually worked. Usually got us panicked and running for safety. We were always playing jokes on each other. Setting up tricks and traps. Nasty little surprises. This time, though, this time they were telling the truth. Turning, I saw a water snake racing my way. Head up, long dark water snake. The next instant, and I don't know how, I was out of the water, up the stairs, in Grandpa Otto's musty tent, curled down deep in my sleeping bag, zipper pulled tight shut up over my head.

How to explain it? What happened next in that cramped, kid sized, zipped shut sleeping bag, my arms jammed tight against my sides? Fish stink. Puke-strong fish stink. Bumps moving round. Agitated, elongated bumps moving around. Slithering round and round my legs and back, my belly and sides. My face. Snakes.

A Father's Choice

Awake and terrified, each of us, each kid in the bunk room in the dark, holding our breath, trying to keep still, keep quiet. Terror logic. Don't move or make a sound and we're invisible, nothing can find or hurt us. White hallway light around the edges of the bunk room door now. Then yellow light from the bumpy glass fixture up over the back door of the cottage. Grandma Maude talking. An angry man shouting. "I'm the kid's father goddammit. I'm the dead kid's father. Where is everybody? It's almost daybreak. Where are all the women with the coffee pots and the doughnuts? Why aren't they down in your boathouse setting up? Where are all the divers, the state police divers and the guys in the search boats. Where in hell is everybody?"

We might have seen it happen. We were all on the front porch that morning. Storm coming so we couldn't be down by the lake. Probably, we were playing Monopoly when it happened, the accident. We kept glancing out at the lake when the sky turned dark all of a sudden, when the heavy rain and the stand up lightning started. Did we see a rowboat over by Eagle Cove with a man and and two little boys in it? Two little boys and a man out fishing, caught in the middle of that storm? After all the talk since about what did or didn't happen out there, none of us can say for sure.

The boat tipped over, the man said. Tipped over when the water got rough. "I grabbed my son first," he kept telling people down in the boathouse, day after day when the search boats were out towing divers back and forth looking for the body. "I had him, too, but he slipped away when I grabbed hold of my nephew. It was only a second or two but he was gone. Gone and nothing I could do about it." Maybe we just thought we'd seen it, hearing the man tell it so often. Tell it over and over, drinking coffee and waiting for word from the search boats.

In the end no diver found the boy's body. It just popped up on the sixth day, blue white and puffed up like a balloon, his face stretched flat. It was Grandpa Otto's fishing buddy found him. He wasn't even part of the search team. Just a guy out for a morning's fishing over on the deep side of the lake. Waving and shouting, heading for our dock, yelling for somebody to come help him tie up. We ran out, three of us, rain dripping off our yellow, hooded slickers. No adults came. Maybe they were bored after all those days of waiting around. Maybe they were talking and didn't notice him waving, didn't hear him calling out. "Don't look," he shouted when we got close, when he saw that we were kids. "Don't look." But we did look. It was too small a boat not to.

Night Swimming

Why, when the lake was our biggest taboo growing up, when drowning the biggest fear, were we suddenly allowed to go swimming on our own in the dark? Let go and not watched? Certainly it was after Grandma Maude died, after Grandpa Otto died. That would make us nine or ten. Did any of the adults come down that first time or two? Did they sit on the beach in the dark in lawn chairs, smoking cigarettes, drinking, and listening for trouble? They must have.

Like any sea change, ours was hard, at first, to notice. Not wanting to lose our new freedom we didn't fight or push each other off the dock or the raft. In that truce world of stars and dark we'd hesitate, one by one, at the end of the dock. Pause before jumping in, our toes bunching up at the touch of those chilly, dew slick boards.

Night swimming. That's when time quits. Disappears. Has no work to do. Every swim, then, is the first swim. Nothing clear or certain. No depth or distance. Unseen things, enormous water snakes maybe, invisible in the dark and closing fast. Hop out or keep on. Sink or swim. Glide, swoop and spin. Balance, upright and grinning, on a single finger, weightless, flawless. Stars, moon, breeze or no breeze. Eyes open or eyes closed. Eyes at water level, blinking frog-regular. The moon is full and bright. The water remembers, knows who you are. Reminds you exactly who you are. The kid remains.

Bullwhip Matinee

Old, black white westerns. Saturday matinee. Lash LaRue double feature: "Mark of the Lash" and "Frontier Justice." Live on stage at intermission, one show and one show only. Lash LaRue in person. Whip tricks galore. Raised on tv westerns, I'd never heard of Lash LaRue. Still, there I was, hot quarters in my hand, pushing and shoving with my big brother to get to the front of the line, buy tickets quick and run in, get close up to the stage. We knew all about frontier justice. Kill or be killed. Code of the West. Cheer when bad guys get plugged. Shot dead in the street. Off a horse. Off a roof. Crouched down behind a water trough. Had it coming, every last one of them. But whips versus six shooters?

Bad guy getting away. Lash right behind him, all in black, swirling a great long bullwhip over his head. Gets close, snaps it perfectly, pinning the guy's arms to his sides, yanking him clean off his horse. Not a single shot fired. Back in town, night now. Lash walks out of the saloon with the Sheriff. Silhouettes, they stand in the street talking something over. Bushwhacker on the balcony all in shadow. Barrel of his pistol catches a bit of light. Lash spins, whip at the ready. One stroke sends the six shooter flying. The next wraps, snake fast, round the guy's arm. Lash gives a tug, launches the polecat, arms and legs flailing. Lands him on his back in the middle of the street. Cheers all around. Clapping, foot stomping. Did you see that? Goddamn, he's quick with that thing.

Lights up at intermission, and I'm off and running. Trying to get first to the concession stand. My big brother sticks around to save our seats.

He has a reputation. Nobody to mess with. If I stay we'd lose both as soon as some bully saw I was sitting there solo. A scrawny eight-year-old, I'm nobody's idea of tough. It's push and shove all the way up the aisle. Same deal at the counter. Mob rule, just like in the movie. Get rude or stay hungry. When I make it back with a box of Milk Duds for my brother, Raisinettes for me, and two watery Cokes sloshing out of wax sided cups

"Howdy, Howdy, Howdy." Buckaroo Bob, weekday host of the local TV western show is talking loud through a microphone up on stage. "The one . . . ," he shouts.

We're on our feet, cheering.

"The only . . ."

Hysteria.

"Lash LaRue!"

Squat pudgy guy wearing a shiny gray suit walks out. Gray beard, big belly, no cowboy hat. He has a thick black bullwhip coiled in each hand.

"He doesn't look like the guy in the movie," somebody says.

"Looks more like Santa Claus," somebody else adds.

Lash stands center stage next to Buckaroo Bob, nodding and smiling, acknowledging our cheers.

On the right side of the stage, lined up all in a row, are four long neck, wooden ponies. Oversized rocking horses. Fat yarn manes and tails. One blond, one brown, one black, and one gray. Tiny, painted on saddles but no reins. Nothing for a rider to hold on to. "Four volunteers," Buckaroo Bob is saying. "I need four brave souls to ride these ponies across the stage. Anybody guess what makes them go? Whips, that's what. No cowards allowed. This is one truly dangerous event. One wrong move and you could lose a finger, maybe an arm or an eye. Anybody out there got what it takes? Or maybe I should ask if any of you Buckaroos wanna win this Family Size box of Chocolate Nougat Nut Clusters?"

Instant howling, arms up and waving, "ME, ME, PICK ME!"

My brother gets picked, then three girls. Lash tells them which pony to ride. Girls get the three closest to the front of the stage, my brother the furthest one back. Buckaroo Bob hands the microphone to Lash for instructions to the riders. "Arms straight at your sides. Eyes forward. Don't move a muscle no matter how scared you get, how much noise the whips make. Keep your back straight, your arms down and you'll be alright. We ready to ride? Okay then, may the best man win." He nods at my brother. "Or," big wink to the crowd, "maybe the best girl."

Crazy fast bullwhips popping here, snapping there, high, low, and everywhere all at once. Quick wrapping round this or that pony neck, giving a tug, hopping free. All four ponies moving, rocking, lurching cross the stage. Right from the start my brother is in the lead. He's on the horse with the black yarn mane and tail, back straight, eyes forward, arms at his sides. One girl is crying, one screaming she wants to get off, and one is riding like my brother, frozen in place, eyes forward.

At the last second Lash lets my brother's pony stop dead, inches from the win. Sudden crisscross whip frenzy too fast to follow. Blink and the crying girl's pony is stopped at Lash's feet. Smiling for the crowd he drops his whips and hoists her down, brings her to the front of the stage. "Cheat!" my brother shouts, running up to Buckaroo Bob, reaching for the box of candy. "I was winning all the way. He made me lose. That's mine." Buckaroo Bob is laughing, guffawing, holding that big box of candy high up over his head. Furious, my brother keeps jumping, snatching, grabbing at empty air. Everybody's laughing now. Laughing and pointing. Then, my brother's gone. Vanished. Two ushers snatch him, slap hands over his mouth, and haul him off the stage.

"Winning the whole way," my brother says over coffee years later. "Remember? I was scared shitless with all those bullwhips cracking and popping around my head. Still, I did exactly what the bastard told us to do. I didn't move a muscle. That box of chocolates was mine. Lash goddamn LaRue. Still rankles. Like that buyer at Conway Stamping does, too. I might have told you about this. Guy tells me I've won the bid, that he just needs a few signatures to finalize the deal. Get back with me in a day or two, a week tops. Contract was already in somebody else's hip pocket. Smile and lie, get you going, drop you in the shit. Fuckit. How about a doughnut? My treat. I just won twenty bucks on the lottery. Your call, little brother, frosting or jimmies? Jelly filled, classic glazed, or apple top?"

Rubber on Wheels

Side by side at a stoplight, engines revving, roaring. "Teach them a lesson?" Fat Leonard shouts. My big brother, riding shotgun, nods. Turning, he hollers for me to "hold on." Fourteen, drunk, I have nothing to hold on to. Below me, cement, the floor having long since rusted out, fallen away. For safety's sake my feet rest on a single, hopping-around piece of jammed in two-by-four. Junker with a crap paint job, a scrounged joke of a thing with a monster engine dropped in. Engine with more power than this stripped down, rattly ass car was ever meant to handle. Beside us a shiny new, daddy bought, big engine Buick. Front seat and back, it's full up with shouting guys. Pointing at us, laughing and calling names.

It's summer 1964 and the muscle car is king, faster the better. Late night in a shut down Shell station. The one Fat Leonard runs. His call when to quit pumping gas, close down, then open up for his friends to work on cars. Allowed, if I keep shut, I watch, all eyes, all ears, as my brother and his buddies turn junkyard finds into hot rods. Dross into dreams. A tiny, greasy front radio with a single, broke tip antennae plays and quits, plays and quits. Somebody shakes it. Somebody punches it. Off and on rock and roll, at no set intervals, all night long. Ragged bits and howling, truncated pieces. Blue air thick, molten at the top of the tire racks from all those cigarettes, one after another. Drained, stomped flat beer cans kicked out of the way, piling up.

"There are," Fat Leonard instructs me, "only two kinds of cars in the world, built and bought. Built cars are righteous. Every piece, every part has your greasy fingerprints on it. Win a race and you own the win. Your dream, your sweat, your nickels and dimes. Bought cars are for rich kids. They don't know Jack about engines. How cars run. They can't change a spark plug. Can't even change the oil. Moron can change oil. Daddy buys it, they drive it out of some dealer showroom all shiny and new. They know nothing, flat nothing about what makes it run. Goddamn crime if you ask me. Come Friday, Saturday night we cruise around, teach these candy ass hot shots a lesson. One day, if you're good, if you keep your yap shut, we just might take you along. Show you how to make a car full of rich kids shit their pants."

Big Leg Ken is a bully. A sucker puncher. Kind of guy walks up behind you real quiet then kicks you in the back of the knees, makes your legs give out. Soon as you drop he has you in a scissor hold, squeezing the life out of you and laughing. Laughing when you can't breathe because of his goddamn big legs squeezing you around the middle, forcing all the air out of your lungs. His father is a fireman. Big ugly guy with a busted up, mashed out nose, and a short fuse temper who wrestles semipro. Big Leg's goal in life is to get a beer company to sponsor him, buy his costumes, then star on Motor City Wrestling. Make a fortune beating people up on TV. His favorite wrestler is Leaping Larry, a short guy with animal thick legs. His signature move is to stand on the top rope in the ring then leap at his opponent, clamp his legs around the guy's gut, drop him, lock his ankles, then squeeze until the guy passes out. Big Leg doesn't have a built car but he likes to hang out at the Shell station late at night, drinking and shouting. After races, when fights start, he likes to step out of the shadows, look some punk rich kid in the eye and frown. Watch the kid turn to jello.

The Bat is legally blind. He has no driver's license. His father, The Fly, does. How the man got one is a mystery. His glasses are as thick as his son's, his sight even worse. When the Bat pulls up behind the Shell station under cover of darkness in The Fly's ancient Nash Rambler he gets a round of applause. Anyone who risks their life in a car for no good reason is always welcome. Story has it that one Saturday night late, well after midnight, The Bat got his wish. He got to drive a hot rod full out. It was on a backcountry dirt road. Terrible place to drive fast, what with the teeth rattle washboard bumps and unpredictable pot holes, but it had the one thing necessary, no cops ever patrolled it. Nobody was going to pull them over and throw The Bat in jail. He's been a new man ever since. Bragging, when he gets drunk enough, how he broke the speed of sound that night, speed of light too maybe.

The Bird Brothers have a car that is half bought, half built. They got it new off a showroom floor but tore out the engine and dropped in a bigger one. A much, much bigger one. They switched out the shifter so they could bang gears with the big boys. They put in reinforced shocks so the back end won't bounce off the road when they take off, snapping the suspension. They've been part of the group since grade school. Twins, they were born scrawny and stayed that way. They have identical, drink straw thin necks and bugged out eyes that look, when they close them, like the bruised eyes of baby birds. Don't let appearances fool you. What they lack in size they make up in sudden fury. Anybody picks a fight with either one of the Bird Brothers, and doesn't throw the first punch, is finished. They don't waste time trading insults or talking back. They snap. Get crazy. Slug the nose, the face, again and again until you're on your back howling in pain, begging mercy.

"Leonard," my brother explains, slipping me a beer, "always hated school. Hated school and loved cars. He started in working here pumping gas when he was only fifteen. Back then he was a real go-getter. Guy would drive in with a fancy car, Caddy or Lincoln say, and Leonard was all over it. Wash the windshield, check the air in all four tires, check the oil without even being asked. Show his respect for the machine see? Did the guys driving those cars give a shit? Fuck no. They acted like Leonard didn't even exist. Like he was nobody. Less than nobody. When he got to be a certified mechanic it only got worse. Same kind of guys show up and tell him to fix their cars. But, they don't know what's wrong with them. Don't have the words to say. To Leonard, see, if you don't understand a car you don't deserve it."

Built car taking off from a dead stop is a terrifying thing to hear. Roars like it's going to explode. Tires squealing, rubber burning, hot fumes everywhere, thunder loud racket. More terrifying is being inside one just then. Light goes green and Leonard pops the clutch. We fishtail, then fly. We're three, four lengths ahead of that Buick right from the start. That Buick though is one fast car. It's gaining, coming up hard on our right. Turning, grinning that maniac grin of his, my big brother shouts, "It's lesson time!"

They just call it "the move." Something they've perfected over time. You're going neck and neck with a trash mouth in a daddy bought, letting him think he can take you. Then, when the RPMs are just right, you bang a gear, shoot ahead, yank the wheel hard right or hard left, depending, landing directly in front of the hot shot's car. That's when you stand on the brakes. Stand on the brakes and watch in the rearview. Kid driving panics, yanks the wheel, spins out of control.

Me, I'm thrown this way and that, all arms and legs, trying not to drop out the bottom of the car, not get squashed flat on the flying by concrete inches below my feet. Then, calm as can be, we do a U-turn and drive slow by the dead stopped Buick on its side in a ditch. Crawling out, crying and puking, were the guys who, minutes before, had been hollering out insults. Letting Fat Leonard know, in collective shouting, what they were going to do to his "shit mobile" as soon as the light turned green.

After that night, I lost interest in hanging out at the Shell station. Thrown left then thrown right, unable to see a thing, I knew I was going to die. Crash, burn, and die. Crushed, maimed, done for. Knew it and couldn't do a thing to stop it. Would I make fifteen if I kept sitting solo in the backseat, directly over a gas tank, while drunk guys with great big chips on their shoulders slammed, stood on their brakes, a crazy fast car inches behind?

The last time I saw those guys all together was at a wake for Big Leg Ken a few years later. He never did get to wrestle on TV. He got drafted first. Drafted and sent off to Vietnam. The Bird Brothers say they heard it from a guy was in the same outfit as Big Leg, how it happened. The Bat says it's a lie, that Big Leg would never die like that. No way in hell. Fat Leonard says it sounds about right for a guy who was always sneaking up on people. Sneaking up and jumping them from behind. Story has it he was working in a field kitchen, peeling spuds, and walked outside to take a leak. To keep the enemy from sneaking up on them at night they used to shoot up huge phosphorus canisters that instantly illuminated an area the size of two or three football fields. That, according to the Bird Brothers, is how Big Leg bought it. He was having a quiet piss in the dark when a spent, thick metal canister dropped out of the sky, killing him on the spot.

Heard an ancient, scrunched down blues singer in a coffee house once. Just voice and guitar, no backup. He was old. Kept falling asleep on the stool, his face drooping, moving for a big, turnip sized microphone. When he made contact, the microphone shrieked. Crackled. Sparked, too, maybe. Made us all jump, anyway. He'd come awake with a jerk and start furiously playing and singing, shouting out one line over and over. "Rubber on wheels, faster than rubber on heels." Perfect, I thought, for the guys.

MUSIC LESSONS

"Hey kids . . ."

Odd place for a rock concert. Odder still for a mock rock concert. Ford Auditorium. Built in downtown Detroit in the 1950s as a showplace for culture with a capital "C." Symphonies. Political conventions. Strictly high toned stuff. Men got dressed up to go there. Dark suits, white, button down shirts, thin bland ties, and shined up, dark leather shoes. Women wore dresses. Below the knee dresses, with matching purses and shoes. Sometimes those funny little white cloth gloves, too. The place had a built in quirk. The orchestra pit that could be raised and lowered. Eighty or ninety musicians on chairs, their instruments at the ready, emerge, appear, a bit at a time up out of the dark. Stopping, eventually, dead level with the front of the stage. Could high culture get any higher?

Times change. The show starts with a tall, rumpled guy standing next to a large gong. He holds a microphone in one hand, a stick-like thing in the other. He has long, greasy hair. He's wearing a sleeveless T-shirt that allows an ample view, from any seat in the house, of his abundant armpit hair. Suddenly a chaos of sounds echoing off the high, poured concrete walls of the auditorium. Whacking the gong fast, over and over, he spins the microphone round and round in front of it. Frenzied jolts and shocks. Amplified assault on our unsuspecting ears.

It's the voice I remember yet, fifty years later. Deep and sarcastic. Stopping and starting abruptly, like his band. "Hey kids," he'd begin, all warm and chummy. "You like ... music, don't you?" This is 1967. Fill in the blank. He did, again and again, with almost every Top Forty group we liked, clapped, danced, and sang along with. Skinny guy, big electric guitar, crazy, bright clothes. Wild, curly, black hair down to his shoulders. Pale face with a looped down, Groucho thick mustache. Centered, as if pasted on, an ink black square of beard just below his mouth.

Was it jazz? For all we knew of music it might well have been. Raucous, loud sounds all at once joining the gong close by and getting closer. Saxophones honking fast, racing and quarreling. Drums in full out furious solo mode. Bass feverishly thumping. Sprung free staccato piano. Electric guitar moaning and buzzing, shrieking. Up out of the dark, slow rising to join the gong player at stage level, Frank Zappa and the Mothers of Invention playing fast and loud. With a slight wave of the maestro's hand, the band quits on a dime. Roaring, reverberating silence. Ears ringing, we stare at the stage, mouths open.

"Hey kids," he purrs. Says something about this being Detroit, home to Motown Music. We cheer, clap, and holler out our love of the stuff. "You'll like this then." Two tall guys, one the gong player, another, equally scruffy, stand before a microphone, center stage, arms around one another's shoulders. Hand flick by Frank, and the band kicks in, playing a perfect imitation of a Top Forty Motown girl group hit. Unkempt, entwined, the two bearded singers are a wonder of tight harmony and nonsense lyrics. It's no song we've ever heard. Somehow, though, it is, just then, every Motown song we've ever heard. Sucked in, we start to clap along. Clap and cheer. Quick hand gesture from Frank and the music quits. Just like that. Up tempo, dance worthy, then nothing. He works the silence, asking, eventually, "You kids really like that shit?"

"I know kids, you like psychedelic music dontcha? Lotsa feedback?" Nodding, he gets the band instantly wailing. Could be Jefferson Airplane. The Grateful Dead. Jimi Hendrix. Taking his time, Zappa moves toward a huge amplifier like he's stalking his prey. Step too quickly and it will sense him coming and run off. Almost touching the ominous front of the enormous thing he spreads his legs, gunfighter style, and rips off a deafening barrage of notes. Instantly they fuzz, crackle, and warp. Sonic bombs raining down, exploding all around us, knocking us back in our seats.

Late in the show Zappa made one of his mysterious hand gestures, and everybody in the band stopped playing, laid down on stage and didn't move. Move or make a sound. Like they'd all, on cue, taken a bite of Snow White's poison apple and gone into simultaneous hibernation. All except the guy at the grand piano. He began playing something slow and beautiful. Was it classical music? Might well have been. He played on and on. After what seemed like a long time that deep voice again, "Makes you nervous doesn't it kids?"

Then, jokes over, a song with no introduction. Propulsive, insistent, relentless. Strong, abrupt images of race riots. Torched stores and shops, homes. Beatings. Hot summer nights with no relief. People, white and black, out in the streets fighting. Mayhem. Violence sprung free, let loose, out of control. TV stations bragging, boasting about being first to show the next horror on their brand of nightly news. Song from our experience. This is late 1967. Short months back, the Detroit riots. Five days of burning buildings, tanks on the main streets, National Guard soldiers in pitched battles with snipers. Whites and black, out in the streets fighting, looting, getting shot, beaten, and killed. Exactly what, his unanswered question lingers, are we doing about all this?

It's that song I remember yet, fifty years on. Frank Zappa's voice, deep and angry, pacing his images, letting them mount, accumulate, do their work. Making us feel what was going on around us. What was really going on. Not the sunny, clap and dance, romance giddy world of Top Forty pop songs. The fact of race hatred. Violence just under the surface. Ready, any next minute, to break out. Let loose. Destroy any city or town. Anybody, white or black, who happened to get caught up in it.

Ford Auditorium is long gone. Busted up years back and hauled all away. Frank, too. Cancer. Sucker punch maestro with his big electric guitar, with that voice, deep, outraged, hypnotic, is warning, exhorting us still. Prescient man, Frank Zappa. Fifty years later and what's changed? What's any different? My nightly news? Yours? Anybody's?

A Simple Thing

The first time through we sang a single word on cue. All of us singing together in a big dark auditorium. It was a simple, hopeful word. Something like peace. Probably it was peace. If not, something close, in the neighborhood. Good word for a dark time. "Pay attention," the skinny man on the stage said. The tall skinny man playing the banjo with his sleeves rolled up. "Each time the chorus comes around, I'll add another word. It's the same word only in a different language." This was 1968 or 1969. We were singing about stopping the war in Vietnam. Can singing stop a war? Stop any bad thing ever? It seemed so to us that night.

We were three or four words into the chorus. All of us laughing and garbling them but trying. Laughing and listening and trying. Then a man stood up in the front row. Stocky guy in a dark suit. He was shouting at the banjo player. Shouting and pointing, shaking a fist at him. I was close but couldn't understand what he was saying. The language he was using.

The banjo player stopped singing, held a hand up for silence. "Friend," he said, "where are you from?"

The angry man shouted out the name of a country in eastern Europe, country behind the Iron Curtain.

"Will you," the banjo player said then, "sing a song with me?"

He started playing a tune on the banjo. Slow and sweet. Like gypsy music. Campfire music. Music to make you nod and smile. He started singing a song in a foreign language. Sang it directly to the angry man in the front row.

I could see the man crying. Standing there in the front row, crying and singing along. Singing louder and louder. Singing and crying, his eyes closed. After that the banjo player said, "Will you sing another one with us?" The man nodded and waited.

The banjo player started the song we'd just been singing together. The one where we had to remember the same word in all those different languages. This time through he added a word from the language of the angry man who kept standing up. Standing up and singing along.

How many times in his long life had he done this, the banjo player? Stood in front of a crowd to lead them in a sing along about something that needed to stop, stop or change, and had angry people shout at him? Tell him to shut up, go away, and quit making trouble?

I'm sixty-eight years old. I was eighteen or nineteen when I saw Pete Seeger stop his concert and get that angry man to sing a song in his own language. Turn a bad thing good, just like that. How peace happens, he was showing us. Listening. Hearing someone out. A simple thing.

Woodstock Story

A snapshot might help here. Crop the scene a bit. Narrow the focus. Lose a few of the distractions. The mud the music and the crowds. The nonstop bustle and racket. I don't have one, but if I did it would show a thin guy smiling by his open trunk, his greased up Elvis pompadour glinting in the hot August sun.

This was farm country. Upstate New York farm country. Dirt section roads, a vast grid network of them, crisscross, connect the whole area. They cut along, between the fields. Link up to larger roads, with small towns. One stopped, dead-ended into another that ran right behind the stage. So forget the famous bird's-eye of the main road in. That two lane macadam useless, invisible under all those cars. Miles and miles of abandoned cars five, six, and seven across, pointing this way and that. Off behind the stage the section road stayed open. All during the festival people came and went. Probably, that's how he got in.

"Hey Hippie," he's yelling. "You hungry?" Who he's yelling at is unclear. His car, a lime green, two-tone, fifty-seven Chevy is parked, pulled off on the grass at the edge of the road. This road is solid people, all baby stepping in the same direction. A million foot, dirt daubed organism shuffling along, slower than slow.

Hard asleep on a patch of mowed grass, in the hot morning sun, I blink awake to a boot in the side, to someone close by, above me somewhere, saying, "Get up, get up and get off of my lawn."

This farmer's house is surrounded by the festival. One section road runs along the edge of his front lawn. A few hundred yards to the south is the back of the stage. In every direction the fields are filled with cars and busses, tents, campfires, and people. Crowds and crowds of people. I am one stranger too many. Goofy from lack of sleep, I stand, apologize, and reenter, become again the shuffle.

A short bit later, hearing the guy's pitch, I stop, step free, and listen. He has a small crowd around him. Dangling, from the top of his open trunk, is a hand lettered sign on a string. On both sides it says, "Sandwiches $5."

"When was the last time time you ate, Hippie? You want a sandwich? A homemade peanut butter and jelly sandwich? They're five bucks apiece. No limit. You can buy all you want. How about you, Hippie? You look hungry, real hungry. And your girlfriend there, she looks like she hasn't eaten in days. How about it, big shooter, buy the little lady some food? Show her what kind of a man you are."

A scruffy little guy in bell bottoms is offering less. Is holding out what looks like a single dollar bill. The pitchman isn't buying it. "Money talks, Hippie, bullshit walks. You got five bucks, you get a sandwich. You don't have the fare, take a hike. No deals. No discounts. How about you? You hungry? You want a homemade peanut butter and jelly sandwich? Talk to me, Hippie? Buy a sandwich or get lost. No window shoppers. I got merchandise to move. People to feed. Don't block the goods. How about you, Hippie, you hungry? You got the price of admission?"

That's when the big guy, big guy with the long, gray ponytail showed up. He looked down into the open trunk. We all did, crowding around, getting in close. There were four large, cardboard boxes, their tops cut off, full up with sandwiches. Sandwiches wrapped in wax paper. Each sandwich was sealed at the top with a price tag. A ragged swatch of masking tape with "$5" written across it in black crayon.

Not speaking, the big guy picked up the sandwich hawker and set him down a few feet away from the car. "Anybody hungry?" he said then, lifting out a box of sandwiches, handing them out one at a time. Eventually, when all the sandwiches had been given away, he put the empty boxes back in the guy's trunk. "You want to help out here," he told the guy, "bring food to share, to help feed your brothers and sisters. That's what this is about, not making a buck, not ripping people off."

Feed the myth? Why not, it really did happen just like that. The baptism, too. Only that happened on our way home. We were filthy. Hadn't changed clothes since we showed up. Five days and nights living in the same sweated through jeans and T-shirts, socks and sneakers. Sleeping on vinyl car seats, in wet grass, in the mud. So we stop in a small town and buy new everything. Jeans, T-shirts, socks, and bars of Ivory soap, three big bars of Ivory soap. The pull off was just where the guy told us it would be, the local guy we'd given a lift to.

"Best swimming ever," he said. "Pull off is by this little bridge a mile, mile and a half out of town. There's a path down to the river. You butt slide down these wide, smooth rock shelves for awhile then the river dumps you into a deep, clear pool at the bottom. It's maybe eight feet deep, tops. You won't regret it, trust me."

Naked, holding our bars of Ivory soap high in the air, we took a ride. Sliding, rolling, washed along by sheets of cold mountain water. Sudsing and sudsing, once we got dropped down into the pool at the bottom, we kept diving under, surfacing, shouting for the cold, then diving back under again.

Baptism? Born again? Abruptly, suddenly aquarians? Initiates, now, to a new way of being? Advance guard, marching troops for peace and love? For . . . ?

For this part the myth won't work. We were just three sleep-deprived guys looking to get clean before heading back home. Back to school and jobs. Alarm clocks and time clocks. Conscription and the Vietnam War. Glad we got to get crazy, get loose for a few days. Nights and days. Got to stomp and shout, scream and sweat at the drop of a hat. At nothing at all. Glad we got to stand up out of that chilly, brim full mountain pool, that deep, green bowl of river sculpted rock, naked and tingling, head to toe, in the warmth of the summer sun.

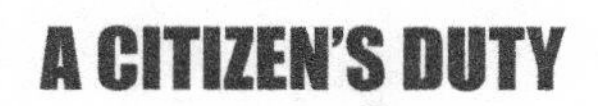

A CITIZEN'S DUTY

Crowd Control

Ants on a twig, for all we could see, the speakers at the far end of the Mall, the Capital tiny and white behind them. Two hundred thousand, somebody estimated later. Biggest crowd I'd ever seen. We'd been standing, shoulder to shoulder, since first light. Stamping our feet, hugging and swatting ourselves for the cold. November winds, bitter and constant, making us blink and shiver, puff steam. There was no room to sit down or stretch out. Hardly enough space to turn around in. People singing and chanting, holding up signs, slogans against the war, doing call and response on cue. Cheering everything anybody said or sang out through a microphone. "Nixon, man . . . NIX-ON," long pause. The words angry, spat out, amplified and roaring over us. "I'll tell you what somebody ought to do to Mister NIX-ON, man, to old Tricky Dick . . ."

The idea was simple. Killing was wrong. The War in Vietnam was wrong. We were dropping tons of bombs daily on a tiny, faraway country. Tons of napalm. Burning, poisoning, blowing up people, villages, and farms. Every living thing. Outrage across the country. If enough of us showed up in Washington D.C. all on the same day and spoke with one voice, the President, the Congress, would have to listen. Take notice. End the war. That was the idea. Citizens speak, government listens. Being eighteen, I believed that.

All that talk before we left Michigan for the March. Life was sacred. Every single life? A child killer's life? A serial killer's? Was every killing always equally wrong? The killing you did, say, if you got jumped, attacked? The killing you did then suddenly, not thinking, just furiously, wildly fighting for your life? Fighting to save yourself, your family, or some stranger who just happened to be there, like you, wrong place, wrong time? Was that killing somehow moral? Okay? Allowable under the grand ethical umbrella where such things got decided? More questions than answers.

Once, when I was twelve or thirteen and home alone, I watched Friday Night at the Fights. It was in black and white. Everything on TV back then was black and white. Emile Griffith and Benny "Kid" Paret were fighting. Late in the fight Benny Paret got trapped in a corner of the ring. All of a sudden Emile Griffith hit him so many times fast in the face, I lost count of the punches. It was as if he was only kept on his feet by the fury of those hits to his head. I didn't look away or turn the TV off. I watched until Benny Paret collapsed, crumpled, and the fight was called. He died a week later. He never woke up, never again saw anything of the world around him. Easy jump, at eighteen, to say killing was wrong. Sport killing on Friday Night at the fights or any other kind. Say it and believe it.

"What somebody ought to do to Mister NIX-ON, to old Tricky Dick, they ought to blow him away. Waste him." Short pause, then loud, raucous agreement. Cheers and clapping all down the Mall. That voice again through the microphone. "And, man, wasn't that great when they wasted Martin . . . when they blew Malcom away?" Silence. Sudden confused silence. "People, you need to get your act together. You want to stop this war? You want to stop all this killing your country is doing in your name? Okay, fine. Best get your own house in order first. It took me what five, ten seconds to get you all cheering for killing? For murder? think about that."

I Get This Telegram

Here's the problem in a nutshell: I'm healthy. It's 1968, I'm eighteen, and I'm healthy. Turn eighteen in 1968 and you register for the draft. You don't register, you go to jail. You register, you get drafted, you pass a physical exam, and you get sent off to war. War in a faraway place. Place halfway around the world called Vietnam. Place I couldn't find on any map or globe if you put a gun to my head.

The draft gets decided by a lottery drawing on late night TV. Same deal every year. Three hundred sixty-five ping-pong balls get dumped into an enormous opaque barrel. Get tumbled and spun. Get picked out one at a time. Every one has a different date stenciled on the side. It never took more than half an hour, give or take, to rearrange all the days of the year. Picked early, you go to war. Picked late, you don't. Simple as that. Me, I got picked right off the bat.

Three weeks later I get this telegram. Official business. Government business. Says I have to report to one street corner in particular, at six in the morning, on a certain Thursday in November. Take a bus ride downtown. Take a physical exam. See if I'm fit to be a soldier. Some time to be eighteen, healthy, and unlucky at games of chance.

I'm crazy in love with this brown eyed girl named Annie. One kiss did it. Goodnight kiss, first kiss, kiss in a darkened doorway. Sprung me free. Sprung me out into some crazy good, crazy vast someplace else. Place I never wanted to leave. Then this.

What do I know about being a soldier, a citizen? I'm only eighteen years old, just turned. What do I know about anything? Before I get this telegram the most important idea I have to handle is what to say or do to make my girlfriend smile, make her laugh.

We take long pointless car rides, listening to loud rock and roll music. We walk everywhere, hold hands, say goofy things, delighted simply to be together. We take picnics in hidden away fields, places where a kiss can turn an afternoon into an eternity. Then this.

Day arrives and I'm running late from the start. Cold November rain. Black dark dawn between buildings. City dawn. Running, squinting, blinking at the rain, soaked through immediately, collar and coat useless.

Too early in the morning, I keep thinking, too early in life.

Fifty or sixty eighteen-year-olds in underpants and street shoes, in socks, we wait on cold, wood slat benches for each next test. We wait in an enormous dim building. What light there is says trapped up by the girders and the skylights, smudging the black roofed sky with no warmth, and no promise of warmth.

Needing sleep, food, clothes, and coffee, we say nothing, hug bare chests with cold, bare arms. Not yet soldiers, we do as we are told. Strip. Sit there. Turn your head. Cough. Shut up. Keep moving. The usual.

One guy is hugging a fat stack of oversized envelopes to his chest, announcing, to nobody in particular, "No way I'm goin' to 'Nam. No way in hell. I got $6000 in doctor statements and X-rays." He's right.

Whatever he or his old man paid for did the trick. Soon as he got to the bad back exam the guy got sent home. Free and clear.

A tall guy with gray skin got sent home. "What'd ya get?" somebody asked when he walked back our way, back toward the dressing room, a home free slip of paper in his right hand.

"4-F," he said, winking. "They couldn't find my heart."

"Piece of cake," a wit down the bench observed, "all ya gotta do to get outta goin' to 'Nam is get born without a heart. Piece of cake."

Eventually, test by test, all the scabby guys and the crazy guys and the guys with bad parts got sent home. So did the guys with doctor statements and X-rays. One long disappearing act.

The group of us left around after that got ordered to get dressed and report to a room down the hall for one last test.

"I'm an agent of the Federal Bureau of Investigation," said a thin, coffee soured voice from the front of the room. The voice was wearing a small, gray face and a small, rumpled, blue suit. "You are about to take the Subversive Organizations Test."

Pencils and booklets were passed around while the bored, little voice explained the rules, seeming exhausted by the effort.

"If you are an active member of any organization listed on this form, make a check mark with your pencil in the box opposite the organization's name. Membership in any of the listed groups makes you unfit for military service, as it is the avowed purpose of these groups to either overthrow or undermine the government of the United States . . . . You may begin."

A while later an alarm clock at the front of the room rang. We were told, then, that our time was up.

"Socialist Worker . . . Socialist Worker . . . get your free copy of The Socialist Worker," came a voice from the back of the room. "Read all about imperialist genocide in Vietnam."

Short guy shaking a fist full of tabloids, moving up the rows, handing them out, shouting slogans, all noise and movement.

Just like that his noise quits. His sound stopped. Two wide and neckless guys in dark blue suits are carrying him away. One guy has a hand over his mouth. A door opens, closes, and that's that.

"Did anyone else," asks the tired voice, wonders the gray face, "check any boxes on the Subversive Organizations Form?"

There is, then, the sound of many erasers rubbing much paper.

A while later, back out in the rain waiting for our second courtesy bus ride of the day, a scrawny kid, stamping his feet, shivering, asks nobody in particular a question. "Where is Vietnam, anyway?"

"Just south of Key West, Florida," somebody offers. "Great place to get a suntan." Having all just been found fit to kill, nobody felt much like laughing.

Instant Gandhi

Swings in an empty school yard. Cold sling seats, late night in early winter. Knees bent, boots jammed tiptoe into frozen wood chips. We're going nowhere, Annie and me, considering my options. No Moon. No stars. No lights close by. What shined, then, shined up, not down. Here and gone snow glint if we looked, blinked, then looked again.

I got a second telegram. Induction notice. In six weeks time I have to report for duty. Show up and start being a soldier. Six weeks to do something, or nothing. Some time too not know, and know in your bones, if The Golden Rule meant what it said. If we really do have to do unto others as we would have them do unto us. No matter what.

Kiss, goof and stroll, get silly and stay silly. Up until then that's what our world of two had been about. Now this.

One option was just to do what the telegram said. Show up. Take the oath. Train to be a soldier. Do what I'm told to do. Go where I'm told to go. Price of my citizenship. Kill people, get killed by people I have no earthly quarrel with.

I could run away. Run away and hide. Try not to get caught. Keep running, keep hiding until the war ends, see what happens. Make no contact with anyone I loved or cared for, anyone who cared for or loved me. Ten years in federal prison if I did that. Did that and got caught.

I could refuse induction. Show up but not take the oath. Say the war's wrong and I won't have any part of it. Their move if I do that. Five to ten years in federal prison for that one. Then there's conscientious objection, the not killing people option. Trouble is it's an all or nothing deal. No quibbling. No yes in this situation but no in that. You have to say killing is always wrong, in every situation throughout history, no matter what. Easy enough to say, but how to prove it unless you're a Quaker or a Mennonite, a guy with beliefs to back you up.

Again, Annie asks me the question I can't answer, the question we've been round and round about for hours.

"Tell me why you're a pacifist. Why you won't kill people. Convince me. And it can't just be because you got a draft notice. It has to be based on something. Some set of beliefs. Something you've always believed in. Believe in more than anything. You can't just say, out of the blue, that you're some kind of instant Gandhi. It doesn't work that way."

Silence in a cold sling seat. Silence and darkness all around. Certain, abruptly, that I'm about to be squashed like a bug by history. A history not of my making, but a history with the nonsense momentum to do anything it damn well pleases with me and anybody else who gets in the way.

I'll See You in Jail

Have you ever had to prove what you believe? Say it and prove it on paper, one word after another? Give examples? Describe yourself doing things, in enough situations, to prove your point? To show that you really do live by your beliefs? My first shot at it was in 1968. I filled out a two-page government form saying that I wouldn't kill people, and why.

Nobody can ever honestly say what they will and won't do in every situation imaginable. So, I told a story. Story about when I killed a neighbor kid, temporarily, then hid under a pricker bush for six or seven hours. This is not what the form asked for. Having no religious beliefs to cite, not being a Quaker, a Mennonite, I told a story. My application to be a conscientious objector was immediately rejected. Here's the story I told.

One hot summer morning I was laying around on a front lawn with friends. We were hot, bored and looking for something to do, an amusement. I noticed a kid across the street. Perfect.

His back will always be to me. He digs, always, in a flower bed along the front of his home. He is digging slowly, doing a good job, a careful job. He is digging with a long handled shovel.

I sneak up behind him, snatch his shovel, and waltz around his yard, mugging for my pals. I have no plan or purpose beyond making my buddies laugh, busting up our boredom with a clown show, an amusement.

The kid does not shout or come after me. He never moves. He always says the same thing. Says he has work to do so could he have his shovel back. Could he please have his shovel back?

That's when I kill him. Hoist the shovel high up over my head with both hands, swing it down hard, hitting him smack on his forehead. Instantly, he drops down dead. Always, after that, there is a terrible sound. A hollow sound. Then nothing at all. No sound. No movement. Nothing.

I run away and hide, hide under a pricker bush in an alley. Hide all through the day. It's a hot day but I'm cold, through and through. Hugging my knees to my chest I squeeze my eyes closed and try not to see what I'd done, try to undo it by wishing it so. Nothing works. It keeps coming back, again and again.

Always, it begins with that brief, terrible hollow sound when the shovel hits his forehead. That hollow sound echoing. Then he falls. Crumples. Still and white and dead on bright green grass. Bright red, thick red blood coming out of his nose and ears.

I cannot change what I did or how I remember it. It arrives, unannounced. Sometimes during the day, sometimes at night. It always follows the same sequence. Nothing changes. I have killed, I am a killer, a murderer. I cannot change that, stop it, reverse it, make it, through wishing and wanting, into something else.

They find me, eventually, a group of fathers and kids. Find me and march me down the block to face the music, meet the kid's father. He comes out on their porch, squinting in the glare of the late afternoon sun.

"If my son dies," he says, "if my son dies I'll see you in jail. I'll see that you pay for what you did."

I saw him drop. I saw him die. But he wasn't dead. He wasn't dead and I wasn't a killer. He was hurt, badly hurt. He had something called a concussion, a very bad concussion.

Nurses had to watch him all through that day and that first night. He recovered. It is years since that happened. I knew, for hours and hours, alone under the pricker bush, that I was a killer, that I had done the one thing that can never be taken back, undone. That will never leave me.

Having killed once, I will never kill again, temporarily or otherwise. I will not be a soldier, and I will not kill people in Vietnam.

The guys reviewing my application were World War II veterans. They never read it. That was the deal in 1968. You wanted to be a conscientious objector, you had to fight for it. Had to appeal and appeal and appeal. Some time to come of age, 1968. Some time, indeed.

Religious Instruction

If killing people was the question, of you doing the killing, and if you got a bit of a pause before any of the killing got started, who would you call for advice? Who is it who can say when killing, or if killing is okay, and why? Eighteen and angry, frustrated, I picked a priest. Figured the Ten Commandments, The Golden Rule, were his turf. Made a cold call, an appointment, then drove off to see what the guy had to say.

I'd been partly trained, as a kid, to be a Catholic, but it never stuck. I never finished the course. Hadn't seen the inside of a church, a confessional, in better than ten years.

Arriving early, I started to shout. Started to holler. Needing to scream, I screamed. Not wanting to upset anyone, I mouthed my rant. Pantomime tirade to an empty, stiff backed chair, a wide clean desk, to a high wall disappearing up into bits and pieces of thick dark books.

Killing people, Father. I need to talk about killing people. Killing strangers. People I don't know. People I've never met. People I wouldn't recognize on the street if they came up and bit me. People I have absolutely no reason on earth to dislike or harm, let alone kill.

Abruptly, a wheezing silhouette in the doorway. Settling my flailing hands, composing my distorted face, I told him who I was and why I'd come. I told of applying to be a conscientious objector and getting rejected out of hand. Wanting to appeal but not knowing what more to say to make my case, to convince a draft board that I wouldn't kill people and wouldn't fight their nonsense war in Vietnam.

He settled into his stiff backed chair and lit a cigarette. Took an ash-tray out of a drawer. Took a glinting decanter out of another drawer. A decanter and two glasses. Poured himself a glass full of something dark, drained it off in one swallow, then filled the glass again. Filled it brim full.

Eyes moist, blurry behind his glasses, the priest looked like the oldest man alive. Weary beyond any power of words to say.

"Let's get something straight," he said, eventually, his breathing, between phrases, like slow crumpling tinfoil, "you don't care anymore about killing people than I do. You're young and you don't want to die. You're a coward, plain and simple. Let's admit that up front."

Filling both glasses this time, he slid one my way across the wide and tidy desk. Lit another cigarette, the stubbed remnants of the first one still furiously leaking smoke, and continued. "Somebody told you you could find an out in the Bible, a loophole. Well, forget it. There's nothing in the Bible and there's nothing in church history to help you. Everybody kills everybody else at one time or another. Always have. Always will. Slaughter all down the ages and blessed on every side. That's your Bible for you. That's your church history.

"You want my advice, say you're a queer. Say you like kissing boys. They don't take queers in the military. At least they never used to."

And that's what the priest had to say.

What the General Had to Say

The General, of course, wasn't really a General. That was just a side of mouth moniker people up and down the block used behind his back. His day job was doing something in the parts department of a Chevy dealership. But he'd been in a war, I needed advice, and he was within walking distance. Two houses down on the right. When you're eighteen and in doubt you take your experts where you find them.

The General had done his twenty-five years active service, retired, then joined the Reserves. Two weeks every summer and odd weekends off, and on throughout the year, he'd squeeze into a uniform and go off for something called maneuvers. "Keeping America safe for democracy," he'd announce to anyone within earshot when he was stuffing an olive drab duffle into his rusted Chevy wagon. "Keeping the beer stores of northern Michigan in business," was the shared conclusion, delivered with a collective wink once he'd packed up and gone.

Sitting on a lawn chair in his basement, I explained my situation. He heard me out, nodding every now and again. When I finished he ambled over to an ancient, bloat front refrigerator and got us two longnecks.

"Your health," he said, clinking bottles.

"What's your old man got to say about all this conscientious objector stuff? Real supportive is he?" the General says, laughing a long hard belly laugh. I roll my eyes, hold my spread palms out. Out and up. We both laugh then. Hard not to.

"Deal is," he began, "when I die, and we all of us die, my funeral is covered. Coffin, grave, hearse, planting, the whole deal, soup to nuts. Paid in full thanks to Uncle Sam.

"I die tomorrow, my mortgage gets paid in full. My boys get a free ride through the college of their choice, within reason, and my wife gets a paycheck every month for the rest of her natural life. Now that's benefits. That's security."

"My life, my life is over. I got nothing to live for. And that's okay. That's okay because I got my bases covered. And that's the main thing, right? Having your bases covered?

"Now you, you're young. You don't think about things like this. All you want to do is chase girls and drink beer, right. Am I right? But when you gonna get your bases covered if you don't start now, start when you're young and healthy? Answer me that?

"I know, I know, I know, you don't want to kill people. Nobody in their right mind ever does. Makes no sense. I felt exactly the way you do when I was your age. Who are these guys to tell me what to do? What right do they have to order me around like I'm some kind of robot? I'm a person see? I got a brain. I can think for myself, thank you.

"Here's the deal. You get in the military in time of war, like during this Vietnam thing, and you get double benefits. You do your little stint and you're set for life. Maybe all you do is fill out forms, unload trucks, something like that. Doesn't matter, you serve in time of war, any war, and you're set for life."

The General nods at his empty longneck, at mine, looks at the refrigerator. I take the hint, get us another round, sit back down in the lawn chair, see what else he has to say.

"Beauty of being a soldier, you don't have to think. You don't got to think about a thing. Uncle Sam, he takes care of everything. He does all your thinking for you. Tells you when to eat and when to sleep, when to shit and when to piss. You do like you're told and everything works out fine, just fine."

We clink our mutual good health, take a breather, then he concludes, finishes up.

"Best long-term investment a young guy like you could make, being a soldier in time of war. Take it from a guy who knows. A guy that's got his bases covered. Got his bases covered and then some."

And that's what the General had to say.

Time's Up

Three times I applied, appealed, to be a conscientious objector. Three times I got denied. Rejected out of hand. No comments, notes, or reasons why, just three strikes and you're out. That's when I did what the rules said I could do, if I chose, which was to request a hearing in front of the local draft board. Make my case in person.

The Dos and Don'ts of a draft board hearing were not printed up and passed around beforehand. In my case they were explained, one on one, a few minutes before things got going.

Alone on a wood bench in a long dim hallway, I was reading back through a copy of my application when the door to the hearing room opened. A tall skinny guy walked my way, leaned in close and told me what was what. Took him one, two minutes tops to explain the protocol for a draft board hearing.

"You got forty-five minutes, that's the rules. We use a timer. Keep things fair. You answer our questions, that's it. We ask, you answer. You say anything, anything at all when somebody hasn't asked you a question, that's it. Hearing's over. Finished and done. Clear enough?"

Who was I to squawk? This was 1968. Countries were dominos. Fight a war in a faraway place or they'd teeter and fall. Turn eighteen and your fate's decided by a lottery drawing on late night TV. Killing is okay and not killing gets you five to ten in a federal prison. So, a hearing where you can't speak, make your case, defend yourself? Why not?

I sat on a wooden chair facing five guys behind a long wooden table. For the first forty minutes or so nobody spoke. Not a word. They smoked, most of them, one cigarette after another. Smoked, flipped through newspapers, magazines. Said nothing.

Then the skinny guy who'd explained the rules to me started things off. Asked me how you stop a guy like Hitler if you don't kill him. How you stop future Hitlers, crazy guys with guns and bombs and armies. Guys who take what they want by force and kill anybody who stands in their way. Guys who'll stop at nothing, will kill thousands, millions, who don't quite fit into their crazy idea of what the world ought to be.

I started to say something when another guy broke in, asked a question. Told me I was in my parents' bedroom. Had a loaded pistol in my hand. Across the room a maniac was coming at my mother. He had a butcher knife and if I didn't stop him, shoot him dead, he was going to carve her up, hack her to bits. So, what would I do?

Bell went off. Fairness timer the skinny guy told me about before things got going.

"Time's up," one of them said. Fair being fair, rules being rules, they all got up and left.

I'm Not From Around Here

The neon dark of the tiny bar was close, dank and frigid. Our group of twelve abruptly unemployed orderlies didn't much care. "Wars stop," one of our lot announced, using his best bad imitation of a nightly news voice, uninflected, omniscient, "when enough people want them to, and not a day before." Cheers all around. The sloppy refilling of glasses.

Up until that morning we'd all been orderlies in a city hospital. Conscientious objectors. Guys working off our required two years of military time doing civilian service. Since turning eighteen we'd all defined ourselves, understood who we were and what we believed, in opposition to the war in Vietnam. Then this.

The day before we'd all gotten the same telegram. Official business. Government business. Told us our stint was over, our services no longer required. None of us believed it. For years the war dominated everything. Defined all our choices. Then, one morning, it was over and we were free to go, just like that.

After a huddle and a few phone calls that morning we started to believe what the telegrams were saying, that we really were free to get up and go. By nine o'clock we'd quit, linked arms and marched off down the street to the first bar we could find.

A window mounted air conditioner was running amok, with much laboring racket, just above my head. Somebody else, unsteady on his pins, was giving forth.

"Consider the nightly news. What they showed and when they

showed it. Early on, protesters were a joke, scruffy malcontents. This wrongheaded war, we were told, was going well. Body counts, our official measure of success, progress, were up, week after week. Then, this spring, there were way too many protesters to ignore. Not just kids anymore. Everybody and his brother wanted this thing stopped."

Pausing to steady himself, refill his glass, the orator continued. "The war didn't end because it was wrong. It was wrong from the start. The war ended because it became the popular thing to be against. It got fashionable to be against the war, so it stopped. Simple as that."

Cheers all around. Much clinking of glasses. Much spilling of beer.

"Democracy in action," shouted a guy off to my left, rousing to the moment. Up and down the wobbly tables we'd jammed together, mugs and glasses pounded agreement to each next speech, to every joke and jibe.

Head knocking from too much beer, too much blasting, air-conditioned air, I settled up and left. Somebody joined me. Quiet guy I hadn't said two words to the whole time we'd worked together.

Squinting, we stepped out into the glare, heat, and stink of the summer morning in the city. That's when he told me his story. Walking along after we sorted out where we were and where we had to go to get our cars.

"Back when I got drafted I didn't know anything about conscientious objection. Wouldn't have mattered if I had. I can't read or write. Couldn't read any of the rules. Couldn't fill out any forms. I got drafted and refused to take the oath. On the morning I was supposed to be sworn in I said I wouldn't kill people and I wouldn't serve as a soldier. They gave me five years in prison. Then, when I got out, another judge ordered me to do two more years. Civilian service here at the hospital with you guys. I'm not from around here. I'm not much of a city guy. I'm from a little farm town up north. Place you probably never heard of. Probably, that's where I'll go back to when I settle up with my landlord. I got nothing to keep me around here now."

We shook hands and wished one another well. City heat wobbled up off the sidewalks and the streets, shaking everything to bits like a fun house mirror. What had we known, any of us, back then, beyond our instincts? In my case, schooled by a kiss, a sprung free kiss to a better way of being. That and knowing how to read and write.

MOUNTAIN TIME

The Great Betty

Two signs, one at either end of the town's main street, say the same thing: More Cows Than People. They're both right. Story has it The Great Betty made this town. Made it all by herself. Started up the one and only industry to ever turn a profit here. In appreciation, her heart was buried in the town square. Buried under an engraved marble plaque half way between the gazebo and the Minuteman Statue.

People who knew her say the portrait is more than just a good likeness. Anyone who saw her in her prime, and there are more than a few left around who did, all say the same thing. Standing in front of that portrait is like being in the same room with her. It's life size. A side view done in oil. It takes up one whole wall in the lobby of The Dairy Breeder's Association Building. The first time I saw it I was just in from out of state to interview for a job teaching English at the local high school. The Superintendent rented two offices on the second floor of that building, one for his secretary and one for himself.

The Great Betty still holds most all the records anyone around here cares to keep. Pounds of milk per day, week, and month. And, of course, the big one, pounds of milk put out by a single dairy cow, year in, year out, for better than five years running. Butterfat, too. Hardly ever a dip. Always right up there where you want it for making the best cream, getting the highest price for your milk.

"I'm ugly," the superintendent's secretary yelled the second I opened the door to her office. "I'm ugly so just sit down and shut up. I'll get to you when I get to you."

Two months later, and after we'd moved to town, Annie and me, I was warned not to walk through a certain farmer's pasture because the bull was "ugly." Knocked him down, busted his ribs, sent him to the hospital.

The Superintendent's office was tiny. The superintendent was not. He and his desk took up most of the space. He was wedged, jammed in, between the back wall and the front of his desk. His belly stuck so far out in front that he couldn't reach things that were more than half way across his desk. He didn't stand when I walked in and we didn't shake hands. "English," he said, starting right in, "you want the English job. Okay, what does Moby Dick mean?"

The principal, a ferret faced man, squirmed in a chair in the shadows. His hands shook. He had trouble lighting cigarettes. "How are you with the discipline?" he asked, a cigarette finally, triumphantly lit.

Deciding to make this quick, seeing that I'd already had an interview earlier that day in a town fifty miles away, a town, unlike this one, where we wanted to live, I asked if either one of them had ever wrapped a corpse.

"Military service," I said, warming onto a rant. "The application says to describe, in detail, my military service. This was during Vietnam. I got drafted but decided not to go. Not killing people, back then, was an option. I filled out forms and applied for it. When I finally got it, became a conscientious objector, I was assigned to be an orderly in a Detroit hospital. Corpse guy on midnight shift.

"Most people who die in hospitals die on the midnight shift. Average Joe and Average Jane, long and tall, double-wide, shroud kits come in all shapes and sizes. Black plastic for men, green for women, and pale blue for kids. If you get rushed, my advice is to at least eyeball the corpse. If you can't measure for width and length, at least do a little mental math. Saves waste. Once you open up a shroud kit, and if its the wrong size, you have to throw it away. You can't use it for anybody else, for some other corpse. Hey, is it true, what those signs say? Are there really more cows here than people?"

"Writing," the superintendent said, raising a hand to shut me up. "Says here on your application that you only have kids write about subjects they're interested in, subjects they know something about. In this town that would be fornication, fist fighting, and shooting deer out of season."

"Hire me," I shouted, standing, slapping a hand loud off the man's desk, "and no student of mine will ever write a paper about anything but fornication, fist fighting, and shooting deer out of season."

I didn't get the job I wanted, the one in the town fifty miles to the south. The superintendent in the more cows than people town called though, said he wanted to hire me. Stunned, I asked him what in the world I said that made him want to hire me.

"Writing," he said. "I like your approach to teaching writing."

Standing in a Field looking Up

Up mountain and hidden away. Marked by no sign, track, or trail. An outcrop with a view, that's Picnic Rock. Climb up and see for yourself. Matchbox houses and barns, outbuildings. A deep, blue lake the size of a nickel. Postage stamp fields, tilled, fallow or green with crops. Odd lot patch of cut back, old growth forest. Squiggle of roads. Logging roads, dirt roads, macadam. Glint, far below, of rivers and streams. Whole towns you could fit on your thumbnail. Purple or gray in the distance, the mountains of upstate New York.

But, you'll need a guide to find it. That and Big Fred's permission. He owns the mountain. Owns the two fields, the old farmhouse and barn just below. Acres of trees surround, protect it. Maple, hemlock and cedar. Birch and junk wood poplar. Boulders big as houses, big as cars block your way. Blackberry bushes tangle your feet and tear your clothes.

There are footprints sunk deep in Picnic Rock. Footprints going this way and that. Four-toed footprints. Three bunched out in front like lizard skin bananas, and one sticking out in back. Claw sharp talons, one apiece out at the end of each fat toe, left their marks there too. That's what caused Big Fred all the trouble. All those funny looking footprints.

Fred likes to stop by and talk. Tell us stories. Collect the rent in person then take us out for short rambles, all he can manage since the stroke, and point things out. Things he says we ought to know about. Appreciate. Mostly, he tells us country things. Why cows cry. Where trout sleep. What dogs know about thunder that we don't. What the sun has to say. What to do with dinosaur footprints. Bust them loose or let them be. And, both sides of the parsnip controversy. To dig, to eat in the fall. Or for sweetness sake, to leave them in the ground until spring.

"Some rot," he tells us. "But some don't. And those that don't, well, those are gonna be some sweet. Special sweet. Ugly, but sweet." Smiling, he adds, "Like me.

"I tell you how I come to own this place, to get my start here as a dairy farmer? Okay then. This was back in the Great Depression. Wasn't nothing great about it, either. I know. I lived through it. Man buys this place. Says he wants to be a dairy farmer. Only he don't know anything about cows. And, he don't like to get his hands dirty. That's where I come in.

"He's a retired professor. Taught at that teacher's college there. The one just this side of Barlow Falls. Says he wants to be a gentleman farmer. So, we come to terms. He lives in the house and reads books. Housekeeper, woman from down mountain, cooks and cleans. Me, I live out in the barn there with the cows. Our deal is that I run the place for room and board. Shares too maybe, if I can make it pay."

"I kept my end of the bargain. Can't hide on a dairy farm. You got cows you got to milk three times a day, seven days a week. No weekends off. No vacations. But I made this place a going concern. Even in bad times, see, people got to eat. They need milk and butter. That professor there, he kept his end up, too. When he died ten, twelve years later, he left me this place, free and clear. House, barn, cows, fields, and that mountain there, too. Let's take a walk."

Stopping just outside the door he points with his cane. "See that ridge up by the top of the mountain? Little strip of brown? Only thing up there isn't green? Okay then. That's Picnic Rock. We're gonna go up there and have a picnic one day. Just the four of us. You two, me, and Myrtle. Soon as this leg of mine," he hits his stiff left leg with his cane, "remembers how to walk."

Shifting, then, from his bad leg to his good, planting his cane, he explains. "It's our special place, Myrtle's and mine. Has been for better than fifty years. From back when we were just courting, first stepping out. I found it by accident. I was wandering around up mountain, getting the lay of the land, stepped around this boulder and there it was, view, footprints and all.

"We neither one of us had much time to slip away. But, we managed. Myrtle, see, she got jobbed out when she was just fourteen. Them Grieves took her in. Worked her ragged for room and board. Cheap bastards. Never give her a dime extra for spending money either. Sold chickens. That was their business, dressed chickens. Plucked, cleaned, ready to cook chickens and fresh eggs.

"It's where we'd get off to when we got a minute free, Picnic Rock. Our secret. Our special place. Couldn't nobody tell us to do nothin' when we were up there. Sometimes we'd just sit back and stare. Stare off like we was king and queen of all creation. We swore a vow to never tell nobody about Picnic Rock, cross our hearts and hope to die.

"But I let slip. Professor surprised me. Jumped out from behind a tree when I was comin' down mountain to start afternoon milkin'. Red-faced and shouting. Off his head. Never saw him so mad. What was I up to, he wanted to know, all the time sneakin' off? What was it? Whiskey? Was I making whiskey? Was I poaching deer? Was I doing something bad that would bring shame on him? Shame or legal trouble?

"So I let slip. Told him about me and Myrtle. Told him about Picnic Rock. About the view and about all those goddamn funny looking footprints.

"Well, wasn't nothin' for it, but he had to see it for himself. Next thing I know he was leading five, six of his retired professor buddies up to have a look-see. They got all excited. Say how they're gonna get dynamite, hire a crew and have Picnic Rock busted loose. How they're gonna have it hauled away and put in some display case down at that teacher's college there. Get a brass plaque on the front with their names on it, seeing how they discovered it.

"Week or two later I seen my chance. It was pitch dark at ten in the morning and dumping down rain. Cold, fall rain. No way in hell the professor was ever gonna set foot outside his warm, dry house. Not anytime soon. So I took twelve sticks of dynamite and snuck out. Set them off one by one sixty, seventy yards away from Picnic Rock.

"When I come knockin' on his front door I was a sight. Mud all over and wet clean through. Mixed my words all up, talked crazy and waved my arms around until he invited me in and give me a glass of whiskey. Drank that off and kept talkin' crazy until he give me two, three more. Then I come out with it. How I was only tryin' to help. How I placed the dynamite all wrong on account of the dark and the rain, and how I blew up Picnic Rock. Blew it to smithereens.

"Holy O Jesus Christ, was he mad then. Called me this and called me that. Told me to get out. To get the hell out. Wouldn't say word one to me for upwards of two months after. But he forgive me. Must have, right? He left me this place?"

He led us, then, Annie and me, on a meandering stroll out into a summer field. Field of waist-high grass. Grass and wildflowers. He stopped, looked up, then looked all around, smiling. "See there?" he said. "See how the sun's hittin' those grass tassels there? Hittin' them, top down? What's the sun tellin' us? What's the sun know that we don't? Today's the day, that's what. Tomorrow's too late. Today, see, today is the longest day of the year. Come tomorrow, winter's on the way. Farm for a living and you know things like this. Know them or you go belly up."

We stood in silence, looking up at the tall grass in the noonday sun. That field of wildflowers waving, flowing this way and that.

"I ever tell you," he said then, starting a slow loop back to the farmhouse, "I had a cousin was born with upside-down kidneys? How we had to drive him down mountain once a week, take him all the way to Burlington? How this doctor there used to hang him up by his heels? Drain him dry with these little red rubber hoses? I ever tell you about that? Okay then . . ."

The Flaming Biscuits of Love

Hard times all over Vermont back when Fred and Myrtle first met. Mortgages due and no money to settle up. Cows, tractors, farms, seized and sold off. Kids lodged with strangers, working for room and board until their parents could sort things out. That's how it was for them in the nineteen thirties, when they were young and just starting out.

The farm family that took Myrtle in had her working early and late. On day one they gave her a to-do list a mile long. Only fourteen, she'd never been separated from her parents, from her brothers and sisters. Cook all the meals, clean up, wash up after. Scrub this, scrub that, hands and knees. Do the laundry, all the laundry, work clothes, sheets and towels, everything, two times a week. Wash it, hang it out to dry, winter and summer, fold it and put it away just so. Dig, plant, and tend the vegetable garden, the strawberry patch. Make treats, special treats, on demand.

Desserts were important. Strawberry desserts were the most important of all. In season, Myrtle picked the best berries fresh every morning, dew still on them. Picked, cleaned, and prepared them to order. Pies and shortcakes, crumbles or cut up in powdered sugar, in homemade ice cream, any way they wanted. Desserts, they let her know, were for family and friends only, not the help. Never the help.

Years later, when all this happens, I'm up early. It's a Saturday in spring, and I'm out working in the wood lot off behind Big Fred's rough-cut sawmill. A broke schoolteacher, I worked weekends and summers for Fred and got paid in cash, paid under the table.

Headlights hopping my way through the early morning dark. Slow bumping across the muddy wood lot. Fred in his pride and joy canary yellow Lincoln, hitting sink holes, spraying mud, snapping branches, twigs, splintery, bark sided pieces of slab wood. "Get in, Schoolteacher," he shouts. "You drive. And don't worry about them muddy boots. This car'll be plenty muddy before we finish up what we got to do today."

Myrtle had always kept a vegetable garden. Always worked it herself. Busted up the dirt in spring with a long handled hoe. Planted, weeded, and watered it. Her job, start to finish. That's how she liked it. Satisfaction of a thing done right. Results you could see, hold in your hand. She didn't ask for or expect to get any help. She liked serving her family fresh vegetables all summer, then having plenty left over for canning, for serving in winter. That, though, was years back. She hadn't kept a garden since her kids left home. The plot was still there, down a short hill from the front of the house behind a thick, close growing row of ancient lilac bushes. A few days before she'd told her youngest son, Billy, that she was thinking about planting a garden again.

One morning early, and telling nobody, not even Fred, Myrtle, her long handled hoe in hand, attacked her overgrown garden. It was tough, hot work. She was sweated through and gulping air straight away. She stuck with it. Got it done by early afternoon, drove down mountain and bought every flat of strawberry starts anybody had to sell. Then, aching and wheezing, on hands and knees, she planted them in rows. Tiny, green strawberry starts in long, straight rows. Hours later, sore all over and sunk up to her neck in a steamy, hot bubble bath, Myrtle closed her eyes and smiled a wide, private smile.

Early the next morning, in the dark, while Myrtle snored and slept, while Fred snored and slept beside her, Billy, thinking to do something sweet and unexpected, ground up Myrtle's garden. Every single inch of it, with his brand new riding mower, the one with that six disc, slice-and toss rototiller on the back.

Fred woke to screaming. Howling. Curses close by, relentless and savage. Myrtle, in the dark, in her nightgown, down on her knees in the ruined garden, punching the turned earth. Her shouts and curses reminded Fred of how they'd first met over fifty years back. He told me the story that day when we were driving up and down Vermont buying every flat of strawberry starts we could find.

He'd snuck in the barn of the farm family she was working for and slept there, planning to ask for a job, any job, the next day. Smelling fresh coffee, bacon, and biscuits, he was walking up the three steps to the kitchen door at exactly the instant she came flying out. Slapping the screen door open, holding a tray of burning biscuits in front of her, she backhanded Fred. Tumbled, rolled him, straight back out into the yard.

Cursing and howling, Myrtle ran on, tray of flaming biscuits before her. Disappearing around the back of the barn, swearing in ways Fred had never heard a girl swear before, she threw the smoldering cookie sheet into the duck pond. It sank with a quick, fierce sizzle. "Knocked me off my feet the very first time I saw her," he said with a wink. "Love at first sight."

By midnight we pulled up to the garden, lights off, a strict vow of silence between us. For folding money, a clean hundred bucks, I was to unload all the piled up, crammed in trays of strawberry starts we'd bought. Then, making not so much as a peep, I would plant them, by the light of the moon, in long, straight rows, same as hers had been. If I didn't wake Myrtle, and if I hauled all the dirt clogged, slat wood boxes away so she couldn't see them in the morning there might, he hinted, be an extra twenty bucks in it for me.

Come morning, Myrtle was not easily coaxed outside, down the hill and around the lilac hedge to look at her garden. Nobody, to this day, knows quite what story Fred told to get her to follow him. But at first light there she stood in her nightgown and slippers, Fred barefoot in pajamas behind her, looking at the immaculate, freshly planted garden. Garden of nothing but strawberry starts. Long, straight rows of healthy, green strawberry starts. Myrtle turned to Fred, her man of over half a century. Wide, tall, and fat as he was, she snatched him up off his feet, hugged him and swung him in a circle.

By berry picking time there were no rows left. The garden, top to bottom and side to side, was solid plants, solid berries. Every plant grew. The plants Billy ground up, the plants I put in by the light of the moon, all of them. And they all produced. Strawberries galore. My job, then, was picking and hauling. Once in the morning, once in the late afternoon. Sometimes Myrtle would have me wash the berries in the sink then set them out on dish towels to dry. Other times she'd have me leave the baskets on the counter for her to deal with later.

One day when I came in with the afternoon's haul, Myrtle was sitting alone at the kitchen table, a three tier, whip cream and berry crammed strawberry shortcake before her. She held a large spoon in one hand, raised and ready. "Fourteen," she said, setting the spoon down and turning my way. "I was just fourteen years old that summer when we all got sent away to live with strangers, all nine of my brothers and sisters. I made hundreds of desserts for those people, the Grieves. Thousands maybe. And never, not once, was I allowed to taste a one of them. Especially not the ones made with strawberries. Those were her favorites. The ones I made with the fresh picked strawberries."

Waving me off, Myrtle picked up her spoon and started slowly, carefully carving out a teetering, three tier piece of that strawberry shortcake. Closing the door quiet as I could, I left her to it.

Some Kids

We are, Myrtle and me, adjusting. Just outside the front doors of the high school, we blink and squint for the sudden brightness. Inside, hallways are dim, shadowy. Steam lingers around our noses, puffs out of our mouths. Snow is pushed and drifted everywhere. Glinting hard in the sun, it has us looking down, looking away.

We are the only teachers with classrooms in the "overflow facility," a two room, tin box trailer set up on cinder blocks. The way out and back is an icy goat path hemmed in between snowdrifts. Strictly single file. Each classroom has its own door. Mine opens a third of the way before hitting the snowbank opposite. Myrtle's opens a bit more, but not much.

The front wall of my classroom is the back wall of Myrtle's. It has a thin blackboard hung on it with two small hooks. BANG. Something big hits that flimsy dividing wall. A desk? A kid? Myrtle? My blackboard hops free, falls. Chalk scatters. Bright, bright sun and things happening fast. Myrtle, in outline, a man sized boy hoisted high up over her head. I blink and she's jammed him, head first, into the snowbank, his legs kicking, bicycling the cold air. "You're no good!" she shouts at those spinning feet. "You're no good, your father was no good and your grandfather was no good." Short, round, and solid, Myrtle is nobody to mess with. "Get this Blinkin' Frog down to the principal's office," she says, her voice dead flat. "I'll meet you there directly."

Free, eventually, of the snowbank, the Blinkin' Frog, a broad shouldered man-boy, says nothing. He has lank, red hair, heavy, red stubble.

Snow crusts, cakes his eyebrows, nose, and ears. He follows me without complaint or comment.

The main office is something of a fortress. It's divided in two by a chest-high counter. On one side are benches for waiting and teacher mailboxes. On the other is the main secretary at her desk. Behind her, behind a door that is always closed, hides the principal.

"Get him out here!" Myrtle shouts when she arrives. "I know he's in there." Before the main secretary has time to reply, the principal appears, florid face and purple tip nose pointed down, meeting nobody's eye. Blurry from hours of slow sipping whiskey laced coffee out of a tall and much dented Thermos, he is in no hurry to approach the counter.

Standing, slump shouldered at the counter, the man-boy is looking down, his eyes blinking metronome regular, his mouth hanging open. "Do your job," Myrtle demands "I told you before, I can't stand to look at this Blinkin' Frog. Bad enough I had to look at him all last year. His no-count father, too, years back. Put him in somebody else's class or I will.

"Would you want to look at this all day?" she asks then, standing tiptoe to twist the kid's left ear, hauling his face up for the principal to see straight on. "Well, would you?" Still standing a safe six feet or better back from the counter the principal agrees that no, he would not.

Back out front we pause, adjusting to the cold and the glare."Some kids," Myrtle tells me then, "some kids are just too dumb to teach. Come parents night, you'll see. You'll understand."

Ribbons

The sudden window showed up one day when we were out. Appeared in a wall at the far end of our small living room. The wall that faces the mountains. It was just waiting there for us when we got home. Sawdust and splinters were kicked into a pile just below it. We'd been renting, Annie and me, half a two-hundred-year-old farmhouse at the top of a steep, root and rock filled two track for a few months from Fred and Myrtle. They lived just across the meadow in a brand new house. "We like looking over and seeing lights on in the old place," they told us when we moved in. "It's where we raised our family."

Forever broke at dairy farming, Fred had money now. He and his sons sold off all the cows, the bulk tank and the milking machines, then set up a roughcut, cash and carry sawmill off in the woods. They built themselves a big new house and split their old farmhouse up into two apartments. We rented one half, a couple from New Jersey the other.

While we were out somebody had drawn a rough window shape, free hand, on the ancient clapboards outside. Drawn it with a fat tip, dark lead pencil. Parts of the drawing still showed when we got home. Parts the chainsaw missed. Rough shimmed into that ragged window shape was a small, made-to-order, wood frame window. Busted up pieces of lathe and plaster, mountain, field, and sky surrounded it. Odd little open spaces all around the frame let in breezes and smells. Clover and cut hay. The spring fed pond. Pine trees and the pungent chaos of untended flowers. A few days after the sudden window showed up, Fred solved the mystery. "We had it put in for you and Annie. Myrtle thought you two ought to have a view of the mountains. I had some of the guys from the mill put it in. You like the view?"

What few pieces of furniture we had weren't worth having. Junk bought for next to nothing at barn and yard sales. Dry joint, tippy chairs and spindle shank wood tables, the finish long gone off them. Our best, almost level table, we pushed up against the wall just under the sudden window. It's where we always ate, looking out at the mountains, at the quick changing weather. It's where I was sitting when all this happened.

I was grading a stack of writing assignments. Seventy-some paragraphs written by twelve- and thirteen-year-olds. Write what you know about, I told them, and be specific. Give me details. "I had a bad day," began one paragraph. Suddenly two enormous milk cows were escaping, in slow motion, through a fallen down section of fence. Fred rented the pasture out for grazing to a neighboring dairy farmer. They were ambling my way, taking their time, staring at me through the sudden window.

A frost sided, galvanized bucket banged down on my stack of paragraphs. Neighbor John from New Jersey, perpetual cigarette dangling, had let himself in, deciding to surprise me with his frozen, steam top bucket. "Women hate rats," he said. "Is Annie home?" Rough pink, wide pink tongues licking the sudden window. Goggle eyes, huge and unblinking, two sets of two, tilted back and looking in, looking us over. Flat black, smashed black sponge noses pressing hard, squeaking against the glass, straining the frame.

"Caught this rat in one of my traps last night. Put the trap in the bucket and filled the bucket with water. Bastard wouldn't drown. Kept sticking his nose up through the trap, up and out of the water. That's why I put the bucket in our big freezer." I looked down into the bucket. Solid, milky looking ice to the brim with a bit of sharp, brown nose tip sticking up, sticking out.

"Well, I gotta go. Get rid of this rat before the ladies show up. You better run those cows off before they trample Myrtle's flowers dead flat." Then, he was gone. Gone too, when I turned back to the sudden window, were the escaped cows. I continued reading, a ring of moisture circling my stack of paragraphs.

"I had a bad day. I woke up late and didn't get breakfast. My Mom made me wear my big sister's dress. It does not fit me and it smells funny. I forgot my math homework. Mr. Williams yelled at me. At lunch I spilled milk all down my front. For the rest of the day I smelled like throw up. Kids pointed at me and held their noses. When I got home I cried. My dad told me to go out and shoot a chuck. He said it would make me feel better. It did. I found a big fat chuck in our garden eating lettuce leaves. I shot him right through the eye with my twenty-two."

The girl who wrote that paragraph is small and quiet. She sits over by the hallway door, ready to bolt as soon as class is over. She wears big glasses and hardly ever speaks in class. Her feet don't quite touch the floor. And ribbons. Most days she has two bright ribbons tied up in her hair. Does her mother do that for her? An older sister maybe? Does she do it herself in front of a bathroom mirror, standing on a box or a stool, something to help her see?

Roughcut

Big Fred's roughcut sawmill was built on a patch of scraped raw, hidden away Vermont mountainside surrounded by miles of deep forest. No signs pointed the way. The tax man and the safety inspector were not welcome. Gouged clean of trees, the land seeped, bubbled spring water all summer long. Pungent, thick black, bark and splinter rich mud caught at your boots, froze you, statue still, if you slowed or stopped. Call out loud as you like, who would hear? Millhands only, guys not much inclined to help. Transients, they lived in rusted out trailers off in the woods that Big Fred let them have rent free. Often drunk, they'd get in fights and wind up in jail. They took off, spur of the moment, to hunt, fish, carouse or just keep on going. Mostly, they didn't call the mill office to announce their plans. When they came up short, Big Fred usually stood them a cash advance, trusting they'd work it off eventually. Not so Miss Caro.

"Everyone lies," she told me on the day I started my first stint of summer work, "kids, parents, teachers, bus drivers, superintendents, secretaries, every damn body." This, she explained, was what she had learned from forty-two years of teaching math at the local high school. Big Fred's older sister, she chain smoked, said little, lived in two rooms built to her specs off the back of his new house and kept the books at the sawmill.

Miss Caro worked silence like a water torture. A millhand would shuffle into her tiny office, eyes down, and mumble out why he needed an advance. She made them say exactly how much they needed and why. Then she'd stare at them, saying nothing, smoking. They'd stand, twisting enormous frayed ball caps in sunburnt hands, shamed and seething. The excuses never changed. Kid needed school clothes, new shoes. Car needed brakes. Wife needed a tooth fixed. "We pay," she'd say eventually, quick, sharp, and loud so they didn't miss her meaning, "for hours worked. We don't pay you for staying home and sleeping off a drunk. We don't pay you for sitting in jail. And we don't pay you for running off God knows where whenever you feel like it with your halfwit friends or no-count relations. No work, no pay. Got it? Need me to say it again real slow so you can understand it? Cat got your tongue Mister Stupid? Get out of my office. I'm tired of looking at you. Tired of smelling you."

Fresh from these humiliations, but well away from Miss Caro's office, well out of ear shot, the millhands bragged about what they'd do if they ever caught up with her when she was out on her own, off by herself. Beat her with a rock, brick or club, anything that came close to hand. Shoot her dead. Throw her off a cliff. Drown her in Fred's trout pond, the river gorge, or Lake Dunmore. Squash her, cardboard flat, into the mountain mud under the wide, bald tires of the mill's one forklift. Three taboos, however, protected Miss Caro. She was a woman, she was an old woman, and she was Big Fred's sister. Hated and feared, Miss Caro was untouchable.

All this happened after I got that registered letter. I made seven thousand bucks that year. Even back then it wasn't much to live on. My paychecks were puny, especially after all the taxes got taken out. My employer, a small-town school board up in the mountains of central Vermont, made a mistake. Didn't take out enough tax. Not for the state. Not for the Feds. Their mistake, my problem. The registered letter laid it all out. I owed the State of Vermont $319.47. I owed the IRS $678, even. Fines, garnished wages, pay up or else, the letter let me know, pronto. How was I, a broke nobody with no savings, supposed to come up with that kind of money fast? We used the wrong formula, the letter said again by way of conclusion. Nothing we can do about that now. Have a nice summer. Recharge your batteries. See you in the fall.

I rented half their two-hundred-year-old farmhouse. It was across a cornfield from their new place and just down the mountain from the sawmill. Knowing the fix I was in, Fred hired me for the summer. Cash under the table, handshake deal. No taxes reported, none taken out. Work whenever I wanted. Perfect for a guy with sudden big debts and routine bills piling up. I had one job, "stickin' pine." Building up drying piles of scrap boards. Bark sided rejects that might be bumpy and ten or more inches thick at one point, then paper-thin a bit further on. Sawer rips, cuts the length of a log until the surface is flat enough to make boards. Those first few cuts, unfit for any use in building, got hauled off by the forklift and dumped in the mud for me to deal with. I laid them out in raft sized layers, put some crossways in between, then stacked them up about shoulder high. They were free to anyone who cared to haul them off to use for firewood. Big Fred's largesse. Part of why nobody on the mountain ever gave people they didn't know directions to the mill, especially people driving official looking cars.

I worked crazy hours that summer. Started before sunup and kept at it until well after dark. How else to get out from under? More often than not I'd be off by myself, building up drying piles for a good two hours before I saw anybody else or heard any sounds of life coming from the sawmill off over the rise. Why, it startled me, all of them showing up like that.

Hunched and resting in the early morning dark on that halfway built up pile of slabs I kept blinking drops of sweat off my eye lashes, too beat to wipe them away with my hands. Looking down, breathing slow. My boots, just above the mud, were thick coated and ripe with it. If I kept this pace, starting before dawn, working late, I could get shut of my debts by late August. Maybe take a week off before school started back up. Probably they'd rot where they were, my teetering, sinking down, slab piles. Unseen and untouched. Pointless work to pay off nonsense debts. Hell with that. Get up and get at it. Be daylight soon. Finish this load before they dump another one in the mud for me to untangle, wrestle free.

Perhaps each of us gets one brilliant moment in life, maybe two. Thunderstruck instant when everything is suddenly clear, bright and simple like never before. Had my one such moment not come when it did I'd be forty-some years dead by now.

Sound of boots moving slow. That's how it comes back to me. Boots squishing down, pulling free, squishing back down. My accuser, when he stops before me, has a sunk cheek, chalk white face. Twitchy red eyes. Black stump teeth. Odd little patches, tufts of black stubble, here and there. A long billed cap of no set color is pulled down level with his spiky, black eyebrows. Three squirrel tails hang from his belt.

Time stops. Balloons out wide and hollow. Things become intensely clear. Vivid. Separate. Glint of quartz. Tiny, bone white twig. Frozen wave of blue black, bark and splinter flecked mud. Large, sunburned men surround me. Each holds a lethal something. Club, pipe, length of chain. They wait for word or nod from my accuser.

He forms words slowly, with effort. "Why?" he manages. "Why did you call the cops on me? Why, Schoolteacher?"

Payback. Guy who rents the other half of the farmhouse. Early on, both of us new to living in the mountains, woke to sounds of dogs and shouting, the scream of bad brakes. Bottles exploding off the side of the empty barn. We walked out into the dark once the men with their dogs, guns, and flashlights disappeared up mountain. "Jacklighting," he said. "These guys are hunting deer out of season. I'm gonna call the cops. Go back inside and stay there. Keep your lights off. If they get arrested, we don't want them finding out who called."

He'd set me up. Must have told the millhands who were there that night it was me who made the call. Me who got them arrested, jailed, and fined. Had their guns taken away. They want revenge and there is nothing I can say to stop them. Nothing they will believe.

"I made a call that night," I say slowly, gulping air. "I made a call but I never called the cops." I wait, tighten my back and shoulders. Will it come from behind, the first hit? From someone I can't even see?

"You didn't call the cops, who did you call?" Chuckles all round.

Milk the pause. Be casual, matter of fact. "Miss Caro, I called Miss Caro. I didn't know what you guys were doing, parking in front of our house, screaming, and yelling. It was late at night. All I saw were strangers with guns, dogs, and flashlights. I didn't know you worked for Fred. I was scared so I called Miss Caro. Told her what I'd seen. She told me to get all the license plate numbers, call them over to her and then go back to bed, that she'd take care of it."

Nobody moves or speaks. Single drops of sweat burn down my back and sides, icy cold, red hot. No air moves. My accuser spits, frowns. Shakes his head. Spits again. Pulls, tugs one foot free of the mud. Kicks the slab pile I'm sitting on. He stares off over my shoulder. Blinks like he's trying to make something out, make something come into focus.

"Bitch," he says finally, ending it. "Bitch."

Weasels

People in trailers came and went. Hid their ratty, rusted out houses on wheels off in the woods or down by the river, worked odd jobs a few months, maybe more, then left with no trace or notice. They were not missed when they pulled up stakes and left. Me, though, I miss one of them. I miss Joanne who wore ancient, leaf-thin work shirts, enormous bib overalls and steel toed work boots that smelled, most days, of cow shit and kerosene. She never said much in class and she settled scores on the spot, settled them with her fists. Half a century on, I miss her yet.

I was teaching ninth grade English when she banged on my classroom door. "I'm Joanne," she said in a deep, uninflected voice. "I'm in your class."

The Weasel sniffed out weakness, vulnerability. That's why I had him seated directly in front of my desk. It never stopped him making trouble, just limited his options. The only open seat was directly behind him.

What did he say, when she walked by his desk? Something about her size? Her various stinks? The dirt streaks on her face and neck? After, nobody could say for sure. One thing all agreed on, Joanne heard it. Heard it and didn't hesitate.

WHAP, WHAP, WHAP. Hard, wet, and hollow. The Weasel, when I turned, was on his back on the floor. Dead or alive, I couldn't say. His face was bloody, his features flat. Standing over him, clenching and unclenching her fists like she was crushing walnuts in slow motion, was Joanne.

While the Weasel was carried to the nurse's office, I listened to Joanne in the hallway. "My Dad taught us that if somebody says bad things to us we should hit them in the face until they stop. That boy said bad things to me."

The Principal was brief, peeking out of his office. Her punishment was up to me. Joanne was my student right? So, it was my call, not his. His door slammed shut. The next day Joanne and I shook on terms. She would, for the rest of the semester, sit directly behind the Weasel. If he spoke when my back was turned, made faces or passed notes, she would stop him. I left the method up to her.

When he returned at the end of the week the Weasel's eyes were slits, puffy, yellow blue slits. His nose was a lump of white tape and thick gauze over a metal frame. His mouth was black and blue. Was swollen shut. He made no trouble that semester.

Nobody ever knew how many people Joanne had in her family. How many people were living in their trailer that spring night when the flood hit and washed it clean away. Washed it away without a trace. This all happened a very long time ago.

I miss you Joanne. Miss you and your leaf-thin work shirts. You and your enormous bib overalls. You and your instant, bare-knuckle justice. Did you make it out of that flood alive? Did any of you? And how many people were there in your family anyway? Six, eight, more? Since you never all came into town as a family, nobody knew. My hope, my hope is that you all made it out alive. Alive and kicking.

Snowmelt rivers flood come spring in the mountains of Vermont. They knock things down, bust them up and carry them clean away. Trailers and people, horses, cows, chickens, and trees. Anything and everything. Weasels, Joanne. There are weasels every damn where I go.

Pastoral With Yeti

Ice storm one week, axle-deep mud the next. Spring in the mountains of Vermont. Nine months pregnant and ready for our baby to arrive Annie announced, the morning after the ice storm, that she wanted her skates. Could I find them in a box marked "shoes and boots" in the root cellar? "If I skate," she said, "maybe my labor will start." She'd learned to skate as a kid on ponds and lakes. "When you wake up and the ice has frozen smooth, no bumps or snow drifts, it's the best. We used to skate all day. I loved it. There's nothing like it, being a kid, let loose with your brothers and sisters, skates on and nobody telling you what to do, when to be back. Figure eights were my specialty. Once I learned how to do a figure eight I did them all the time. It made me, when I did a good one, feel like I was the most graceful person in the world."

Bright sun that morning, glaring off the ice. Inches of ice on everything. Fence posts, trees, furrows, and corn stumps. "Its been a while but if I find a level place I'm going to do a figure eight," she said, skates on, wobbling out the kitchen door. Gliding off, around that frozen corn field.

A week of rain followed. Cold, steady rain. The ice melted, rivers over flowed, fields seeped. Deep mud and standing water everywhere. The dirt two track up to our place from the main road was a washboard of ruts and running water. Slow road in good weather, slower than slow now. Big rocks and thick roots, once hidden, banged the bottom of our car, tilting us this way and that, even when we were just inching along. Still, no baby.

Broke most of the time, we made do with what we could scrounge at barn and yard sales. We found an antique brass bed, dented, discolored but, by our lights, an amazing find. Held together by two bent metal side pieces it wobbled and shook but somehow stayed upright. The heat in our bedroom came up through a small, ornate, metal grate in the floor from a secondhand Franklin Stove. We bought it knowing nothing of wood stoves. It only gave off heat if you were right in front of it feeding in wood. We couldn't bank it for the night. Leave it untended for more than an hour, no matter how big the fire you'd made, and it went stone cold. For warmth we had a pile of old quilts. Across the room, on a tiny table, was a bad, old, black and white TV. We got three stations, off and on. When it got dark that spring we'd get in under our heaped up quilts and watch any show we could find. Any show that didn't dissolve, disappear into static and snow.

"Musky," one guy said, scrunching has mouth and nose up like he could smell it still. "Like a week old bait box. Like corn gone bad in a silo. I sure in hell smelled it before I saw it."

"Humanoid," said the round faced woman in the checkered hunting cap. "Upright and walking just like you and me. Only with those long arms hanging down and hairy all over like some kind of ape. Only it wasn't no ape. Not here in the Cascades it wasn't. It was a Bigfoot. I seen it with my own eyes. Believe it or don't. I know what I saw. I know what I heard. When it seen me it run off. It was screaming too. Screaming in this high-pitched voice like a trapped rabbit, like a little girl. Give me the shivers. Made every single hair stand up on the back of my neck. On my arms and legs too."

"Pendulous breasts," said a frowning man, unsmiling under a severe flattop haircut. "It had gray, pendulous breasts. Swinging this way and that like they was in slow motion. Never forget it long as I live. That and the stink. Smelled like a swamp."

We busted up laughing. Crying for laughing. Pounding the quilts laughing. Then Annie's water broke. Just after the guy on that "Truth is Stranger Than Fiction" show about Bigfoot sightings described those slow swinging, gray, pendulous breasts. I will not describe our stop and start creep down that washboard two track in the starless dark.

Or having to drive crazy slow round the north shore of Lake Dunmore because of all the switchbacks. Or how thick fog settled in just when we made it out to the main road north, twenty-eight miles away from the only hospital.

Our spring baby arrived a few hours later, a fine bright rooster crest of red hair running along the middle of his head. Silky fine, upright, red hair. Prompted out into the world not by ice skating round a frozen corn field, not by any trick we dreamed up to coax him out, but by laughing. Delightful, head to toe laughing.

Requiem for Rooster Boy

"Hit him," the man said. A big guy with a scald red face and big, purple red hands. Wadding a sun bleached ball cap, he looked uneasy under the bright lights of my classroom. It was Parents' Night, my first. We'd just met. I was new to teaching, to living up in the mountains of Vermont. "Talk to Bucky," I said. "Get him to quit jumping up in my class whenever he feels like it. Jumping up and crowing like a rooster."

"He acts up again, hit him," he told me, turning and walking out. If I'd known what he was going to go home and do, I never would have mentioned it.

Bucky was big for his age, at thirteen. Tall and thick. Always needing a shave. He'd worked since he was little. Out in the woods helping his father cut trees in all kinds of weather. Cut, trim, and skid them. Haul them off to sell at roughcut sawmills for cash in hand. Trees they owned the rights to and, rumor had it, trees they didn't. Trees, maybe, cut quick when nobody was looking. Trees around big summer homes that were set back, hard to see from the main roads.

Bucky liked to scare other boys. Mouse them down. Make them shake and twitch. He had thick brown hair hanging down over his collar and his ears. Over his eyes. His hair was part of it. He'd turn fast in his seat, push the hair up out of his eyes, taking his time, not blinking or smiling, then stare a kid down. Letting the kid know. Putting him on notice. I might beat you up. Maybe today. Maybe tomorrow. Maybe never. Think about that. Think about that and sweat. Lose sleep.

His clothes were a part of it too. He always wore black. Head to toe black. Tight, black jeans and T-shirts. Black, steel toed boots with bits of metal showing through. A wide, black leather belt with a heavy, square, metal buckle. Did he use it in fights? One teacher said he did. Said he saw him snatch it off out by the bus when he was jumped by a group of boys, swinging the buckle at their heads to clear himself a path, even up the odds.

Rough justice. Got what he deserved. Serves him right. Only thing a kid like Bucky understands. Lunchroom teacher conversation the day after Parents' Night. I found out what they were talking about when Bucky showed up for my class that afternoon.

He came to the door of my class and waved me out into the hallway. The eyes. That's all I recognized. That and the general shape, bulk of him. Chalk white, cue ball head. All his hair hacked, gouged off. A few tiny bristle patches all that was left of it. Streaks of dried brown blood where his father had at him. With what? Dull scissors? Sheep shears?

Gone, too, was the outfit. The uniform. The look. In its place a garish Sunday get up. The shoes, mouse brown. A baby blue, sponge cloth, polyester suit. A smudged, button up, white shirt and a thick, knotted, wide, bright tie. Tie with blurry red, green, blue, and yellow flowers the size of grapefruit all over it.

"Don't ever," he pleaded, looking me in the eye, a shake, catch in his voice, "say I done bad things in your class to my Old Man. He has a temper on him. He gets started, can't nobody stop him. I'll do whatever you say from here on out, only you got to promise, swear you won't rat me out again."

We shook on simple terms. No crowing. Assignments in on time. No stare downs. No pushing, shoving, or tripping. No fights on school grounds. Flat none.

Bucky was as good as his word. A month or so later, his hair starting to grow out, he raised his hand. Offered to read his paper. Still wearing the Sunday get up, the suit and shoes, the shirt and tie, he stood up and read.

"I was home, sick. I had the flu. Fever and sweats. Puking and seeing things. I hear my dog barking. He's going nuts. I look out my bedroom window. It's Fat Kennedy, the mailman. He's poking my dog in the face with a long stick and laughing. My dog is old. He's blind, too. He's at the end of his chain, jumping and barking. He can't get at Fat Kennedy. He can't see him and he can't fight back. Next day I have a little surprise for Fat Kennedy when he comes around. I unhooked my dog's chain up by our front door. When Fat Kennedy kicks dirt in his face he jumps him. Knocks him down. Bites him on the ass and won't let go. I laughed and laughed. Served the fat bastard right. The end."

Bucky never graduated from high school. He dropped out at seventeen and joined the Marines. Lied about his age. Big as he was nobody asked any questions. One day after he'd finished up basic training, and just before he deployed to Iraq, he came by the school for a visit. He told me he was sorry for being a pain in the ass all those years ago in my class. For jumping up and acting out all the time when I was trying to teach. Jumping up and crowing like a rooster. That he was a man now, a Marine, and he understood how important it was to follow orders. To do what you were told. Said he was just stopping by to make things right before he left.

I told him we were square, the two of us, and that we had been for a long time. That I never would have told his father about the crowing if I'd known he was going to go straight home to hack all his hair off. Hack his hair off and make him dress like a clown for the rest of the semester.

Was it a month later I was at Bucky's funeral? Seemed much shorter than that. Anyway, I was at his funeral sitting in a pew next to his father. "Ambush," he told me. "His first patrol. Killed the whole lot of them. We were saving up. He was sending me his paychecks all through basic. We were going to use the money to buy a new skidder, maybe a few wood lots up mountain we'd had an eye on for awhile. I don't know what I'm going to do without him."

At first he only did it when my back was turned to the class, when I was writing on the blackboard. Later on, and just before that Parents' Night, he'd do it any time he felt like it, whether I was facing the class or not. He'd stand up slow and easy, taking his time. Nodding politely this way and that as if to acknowledge the coming applause of his many fans, his loyal following. First he'd tuck his hands back up under his armpits, then flap his wings. Eyes shut, head shooting up and back, up and back, prancing, he'd start to crow. Crow and crow. Loud and long. Just like a real live rooster.

SCUFFLING FOR COIN

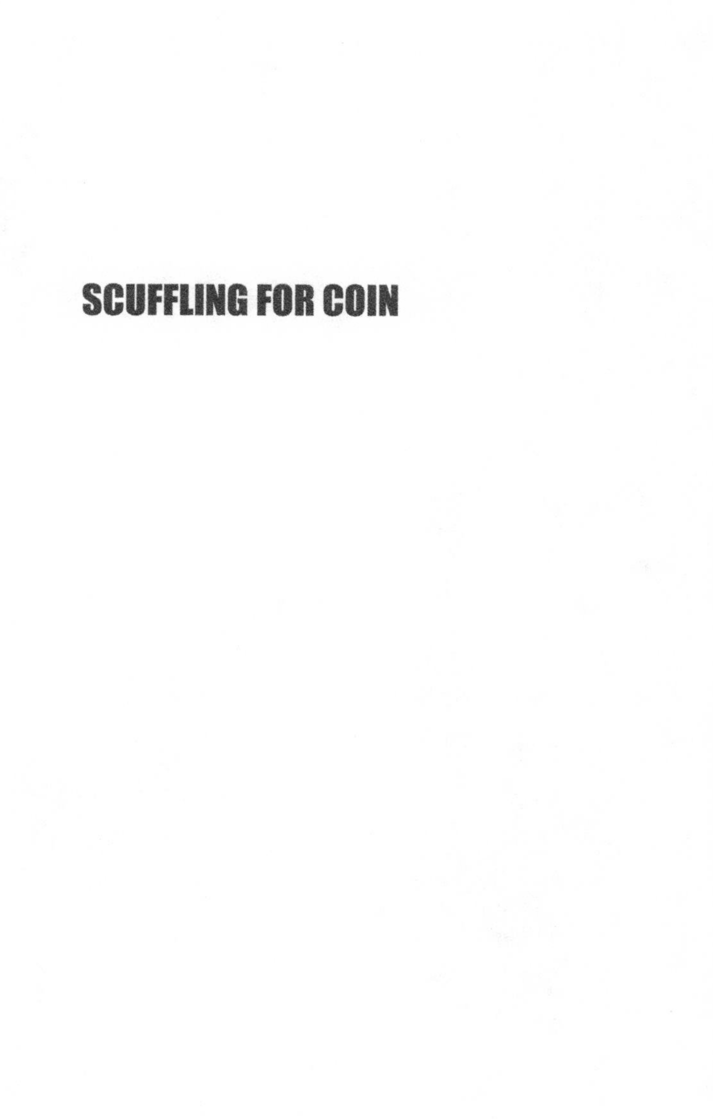

War Stories

Feet all week. Covered up, tied up, and roasting. Slow roasting in dark socks, oven socks. In thick leather, black leather shoes. Man shoes. Salesman shoes. Wing Tips. Absolute worst week to work the city. Cold calls and cold shoulders. Heat wave that never let up. Breeze, cool or otherwise, that never once blew. Finally Friday. One stop, one last stop and I'm home free. Give the old man his groceries and leave. Unload the bag, tell him what I bought, say his list out loud and go. Get home. Get out of the man clothes. Lose the suit and tie, the sweated through undershirt, the rumpled pants, the socks, and shoes. Breathe.

Don't let him start a war story. He starts a war story, I'm stuck. Did nothing but World War II ever happen to him? My mom, his better half for over fifty years, recently dead? All his jobs, selling this, selling that? His parents? His brothers and sisters back in Oklahoma? Our family? A tornado? A fist fight? A close call car crash? Nothing? Nothing but World War II? Slap me awake at midnight, at one, two, three in the morning. Give me no coffee. Give me no more than five seconds to wake up. It won't matter. I will recite his World War II stories word for word, pause for pause, every last one of them. Sit me upright and I'll do the hand gestures too.

Unloading his order, saying it, item by item. Denture cream, not the powder, the creme. Three bananas, not green but not too brown, either. Yellow all over. Two cans baked beans, store brand. Six rolls toilet paper, store brand. One jumbo bottle no-name cola. Box of gingersnaps, the hard kind, not the soft. Never the soft. They get stuck in his dentures. Pound of bologna that's on sale this week, thin sliced for frying. For when he craves a fried bologna sandwich at midnight or one in the morning.

Trouble. He didn't say hello. Didn't get up out of his tilt back easy chair, shuffle over to supervise. He starts right in. "It was a hell of a shot. Shot to be proud of. People commented on it. The distance. The angle. Those big jungle leaves between me and the Nips."

It's his "popping a few Nips, shooting fish in a barrel" story. How many times do I have to hear him tell it? A thousand? A thousand and one? I interrupt. Hold my hand up and interrupt. Maybe he sees my hand held up for silence, maybe he doesn't. He's ninety, legally blind, and mostly deaf. I move to the center of the room, talking loud and fast. Stopping him from saying one word more.

"World War II, the Philippines, the Island of Samar. You and two buddies are out on patrol in the jungle. One guy, Shannon, a big old boy from Chicago. He likes to drink, fight, and have his way with native gals. The word, Dad, is rape. And when, exactly, does a girl become a gal, get to be fair game for you and your buddies? Ten, eleven, twelve? The other guy, Stokes, is a long, tall drink of water from Georgia. He'd never been more than ten miles from home before the War. Always says he'd give his left nut for one taste, just one little taste, of his momma's homemade peach ice cream. Hand churned, homemade peach ice cream. I leave anything out, Dad? That about it so far? Good."

Silent, he stares in my direction. What he sees, what he hears I cannot know. I keep talking loud and fast. I will not let him start back up. Not today. Finish and leave. Get home, get out of these clothes. These goddamn shoes and socks.

"At the bottom of a steep hill, a good 200 yards away, and mostly blocked by big jungle leaves, six naked men bathing in a river. Japanese soldiers, their uniforms, their gear and guns, on the far shore, well out of reach. Hard shot. But, like you always say at this point, Dad, 'no hill for a climber,' short pause, big grin, 'just like shootin' fish in a barrel.' You spotted them. Saw them first. So, you get to pick. You get first shot. You point at yours, your buddies nod and wait. Unspoken protocol. BANG.

Yours drops like a sack of potatoes. Why not a sack of beets or onions, Dad? Why always a sack of potatoes? Single shot. Clean shot. Head shot. BANG. BANG. Stokes and Shannon drop theirs. Taking turns now you finish off the remaining three. Always, just before you 'pop' them, never shoot, always 'pop' them, they stand, unmoving and wide eyed, like deer caught in headlights. So what are they, Dad? Nips? Deer caught in headlights? Fish in a barrel? Does it make your story somehow better if you don't call them what they are? What they were? Six naked, unarmed men bathing, washing up in a river?"

"See!" he shouts, as I turn to leave, start for the door. "He can't stand to be in the same room with me for more than five minutes."

Stuck in bumper to bumper I hear an ad on my car radio. Late afternoon and the heat won't quit. Won't let up. Still no breeze. Stinks surround me, seeping in, staying put. Hot grease stink of hamburgers and french fries. Cigarette smoke. Bus exhaust. Ripe garbage. It starts off, this ad, with a famous electric guitar solo. I turn up the volume. Pure reflex. Anthem when I was coming up. Nose thumb, who are you to tell me how to live my life anthem. Cut, now, and pasted into a sales pitch. Intro for a package deal guaranteed to deliver the authentic tie-dyed goods. To recreate, for a fee, a bit of the original magic. All major credit cards accepted.

Suit still on, I'm standing in the middle of my oldest son's bedroom, shouting. My noise on the subject never changes. Set piece rant. His bedroom walls are covered with my mementos. In a plastic baggy, my unused tickets for all three days. That special edition of Life Magazine I bought after I got back home. The double album folded out, pinned up. Three part crowd shot, sepia tint, of thousands drenched and dancing.

Had he heard the ad on the radio? Did he know what some con man promoter was promising to deliver? "Look!" I shout. "I didn't use those three tickets, because Woodstock wasn't about tickets. About making a buck. Turning a profit. It was about sharing. Looking out for one another . . . . "

"I know, I know, I know," my son says, holding up a hand, stopping me cold. "Woodstock was about living in the moment, right? Look, Dad, I've heard this all before. Heard it a million times before. So some guy wants to put on a three day concert in upstate New York and call it Woodstock II. So what?

"Every time you hear somebody trying to sell anything to do with Woodstock you get like this. You go nuts. Turn into a crazy man. You don't own it, Dad. Woodstock is not your private property. Thousands of other people were there, too. Thousands and thousands of other people. Who says your version is the right one? The authentic one? The one and only? What if somebody had the absolute worst time of their life at Woodstock? What about that? Didn't people die there? Didn't some people get rolled over by big trucks when they were snoozing in their sleeping bags? Who was looking out for them?"

I slam the door to his bedroom on the way out. Slam it hard as I can. I want to hear things falling off walls, glass breaking, wood splintering. Hours later, barefoot, finally, I slouch under our ancient apple tree in my sprung seat lawn chair, something I'd been meaning to fix. The dew wet grass is long and falling over. Something else I'd been meaning to do. The grass is cool under my feet, between my toes. The sky is going dark. I should stand up, walk back inside and put things right with my son. Apologize. I stay put.

A single fat drop at the top of my long neck beer bottle stands still, catches a fierce quick glint of last light. Wobbles, then drops fast down the neck of the bottle and over my knuckles. When, I wonder, did I become my Old Man? Maybe it started with the shoes. That very first pair, bought after I quit teaching. Once I decided to make some "real money." Got them in the men's section of a department store. Figured I needed the look, the gear, same as my Old Man had back when he was driving all around, selling this, selling that. All those funny little holes punched into his shoes. Punched in but not through. Just for looks. Not for cooling feet, that's for sure. Thick leather, black leather shoes. Man shoes. Salesman shoes. Wing tips.

Pitchman's Blues

A while ago in winter, broke and between things, I signed on with the U-Need-It Novelty and Notion Company, Inc., a drive your own car, cover your own expenses, strictly commission outfit out of Elkhart, Indiana, bought a road atlas, and headed straight north into Michigan's Upper Peninsula. It was not a job I wanted to die for, selling seasonal gimcracks, bulk rate, to mom-and-pop variety stores in tiny, one-horse towns up along the Canadian border. But, it wasn't a job I wanted to starve at either. All of which is why, late on a well below zero afternoon, after striking out in Paradise, then striking out in Seney, I drove north out of town down a quickly disappearing stretch of drifted over macadam.

Steady falling all day, the snow suddenly started dumping down, getting worse. Both sides of the road were drifted up ten, twelve feet. I hadn't been driving more than an hour, hour and a half, when the sun quit. My windshield went flat white. No depth, no distance. Big thump. Then nothing. No forward, no reverse, nothing. Stuck, axle deep, my choices got simple. Stay put, hope for help, freeze in my car. Go out into the blinding white, try to find help, freeze outside.

Nothing I had on, hat, suit, shoes, or coat was up to the weather, would keep me alive all night long in wind that was an easy twenty below zero and dropping fast. I hadn't packed or planned for this. No flashlight, flares, blankets, CB radio, food, or water. I set off walking.

Walking blind in a blizzard. Fat flakes, snapping this way and that, kept me blinking, looking down.

A long or short time later, I have never known which, the storm paused. Momentarily quit. In that brief, still moment I saw a smudge of light on the dark of the distance. To my delight and salvation, Sulo's Fish of the World Restaurant, a Diner With a Difference, is amply announced, in dim and dark, by enormous neon fish. The largest, a walleye the size of a small tuna, is afloat above the main entrance with the promise of GOOD EATS flashing from its belly. Two dog sized rainbow trout leap, wiggle, and straighten across the front two windows, booth- and counter-high. Letters leap with them, spelling out the name of the place in humming ,bright, rainbow colored neon. Sulo, the cook, owner, builder, and sole employee of the place, is a wizard with berry pies, beer battered fish, and onion fried spuds.

Up and down the fish patterned counter elbow islands shone white with use and welcome. A wide, tall percolator gargled and puffed steam. After I'd eaten a heaping fish and chips dinner, with cole slaw, with roll and butter, finished a large piece of thimbleberry pie a la mode, and was on my third cup of hot, black coffee, Sulo explained his theory of attractions. "There's only two kinds," he told me, "there's natural, and there's man made. The Mystery Pit outside Bark River and Snakes Alive just north of Grayling, those are man made. Somebody dreamed them up. Saw them in their mind's eye then made them happen. Built them up out of nothing. Nothing but an idea. Grand Canyon, Munising Falls, Snout Point Narrows, those are all natural attractions. Fish of the World is one hundred percent man made. I dreamed it up and I built it. Wasn't for me, there wouldn't be No Fish of the World. No Fish Room either.

"Show you what I mean," Sulo said then, walking to the far end of the counter, nodding for me to grab my coffee and follow along. He disappeared through a long set of dark curtains. The Fish Room is announced, just move those curtains, in bright blue neon. Stepping through, I stopped abruptly. Couldn't see a thing. Bright diner one instant, black dark nowhere the next. Blinking, adjusting, I started seeing fuzzy slabs of purple light stacked up along the walls. Then fish and bright stones. Lots of tiny fish swimming around, jewel bright stones heaped up beneath them.

Sulo had rigged the room with floor to ceiling fish tanks lit by black lights. He wanted you to feel like you were under water. The trick worked. "What," he asked me then "is the worst thing happens in a restaurant after your order's in? You get bored, that's what. Bored and restless. You got kids with you, they get bored, too. Kids or old people. Trouble. Bickering starts in. Pick, pick, picking. Arguments, maybe a fight. Solid mess any way you look at it. Nobody gets bored at Fish of the World. Nobody, but nobody. That's why I call it a Diner With a Difference.

"I got fish here from all over the world. I got fresh water tanks and I got salt water tanks. I got puffers, scats, flora doras, tinfoils, angelfish, the works. I got barking fish, walking fish and one fish you can see right through. You name it, I got it."

That's when he motioned me across the room to one tank in particular. Standing close, I couldn't see a single fish. There was a bright bed of colored rock chips, a bubbling water jet in one corner, a tiny kettle headed diver nodding and nodding over a sprung top treasure chest, but no fish anywhere. Putting a finger to his lips for silence, Sulo reached down into the front pocket of his apron. Winking in the purple glow he opened his hand, showing me what looked like three lopsided grapes. "Chicken hearts," he whispered. "I get them out of the gizzard packs when I buy whole frozen chickens by the case load. Always buy bulk for best price, that's my motto. Now watch this."

Tilting his left hand at the top of the tank, he slow walked the fingers of his right hand behind the chicken hearts, herding them, one by one, down to the water. When the first two dropped in the water they just sank. Wobbled and sank. That third chicken heart though, it got caught in a column of bubbles and stayed up by the top of the tank, hopping and rolling. Then, too fast to follow, it got snatched. Bitten clean in two.

"When it happens," Sulo explained, "it happens fast." The ragged remains of the third chicken hearted sank to the bottom. Two tiny brown fish the size of a child's thumb hid behind a clump of fake, bright green seaweed. "Dwarf piranha," he explained. "They come all the way from the Amazon River. School of them can take a full grown cow down to bones in seconds flat."

Exactly what, I wondered, standing there in the glow of Sulo's underwater world, had I ever dreamed up? Dreamed up and made happen? Pitch, maybe, for this or that line of pointless products? Talk, talk, talking, that's all I did for a living. Talking too much. Trying to string strangers along long enough to set the hook, catch their interest, make a sale, make a few bucks.

"Don't be a sink easy," they told us in sales training at U-Need-It. "Believe in yourself and the world will, too. Your car, that's not just a car, that's your Opportunity Mobile. The only limit, absolutely THE only limit, to how much you can earn, that's simple. It's deciding, up front, how much money you want. Deciding then going out and getting it. Doing whatever it takes to make it happen. Hit the road runnin', gentlemen. We'll find out what you're made of, which of you pack the gear and which of you are outta here, come bonus time."

Dime Store Belts

Afloat, alone, and furious still. Far, far out from shore. Arms, legs, going thick, getting heavy with the cold. No moon or stars. Only the dark. Everywhere, the dark. Black, deep mountain lake. Late September. No hints of dawn. No leak of light. Not through the pine tops or round the boulders high up on the ridge. Not from the lodge or the cabins far back behind me.

Stopped, spent, and treading water. Bottomless, black water. Blinking, looking around, screaming. Screaming for all I was worth, again and again, face under water. Curse, shriek, and howl, face under water. Trouble the fish, not the air, with my troubles. Clams if sounds got down that deep, clams and crayfish. Twenty-seven years with the same company and they fire me with a letter. Not a phone call with a voice on the other end. No sit down, face-to-face chitchat. A one page letter. Three paragraphs. Details of your severance to follow. Short and sweet. Company logo on top, signature at the bottom. Signature of nobody I know.

Who writes a letter like that to a perfect stranger? Writes and signs it? Dump a geezer? No problem, Boss. Consider it done. Letter written and out the door. Anything else I can do for you while I'm at it? Did he, I wonder, ever carry the bag, this punk letter writer? Did he ever build up a territory out of nothing? Sweat a big sale to make quota, to get a monthly commission check anywhere close to covering all his bills? Fuck him. Fuck him and the horse he rode in on.

Tiny, yellow lights. Pin dot lights. Windows from the lodge? The cabins? Here and there scatter now of fuzzy gray bits. All those lined up, overturned, aluminum canoes at the far end of the beach? Too dark yet to tell. Too dark and too far away.

Scalp prickle. Something behind me. Big, behind me, and close. Turning slow, heart banging in my throat, my chest. Demon red eyes, two feet away. Unblinking, staring me still, freezing me in place. Long, black, razor, dark beak. Massive, black head. Nightmare, fairy-tale loon come alive out of some antique book, come to pluck out my eyes, snip off my nose, teach me a lesson?

I'm talking now, quiet and slow, trying to keep the shakes, the shudder out of my voice. "Please don't hurt me. I mean no harm. No disrespect. Look, I was just blowing off steam. Venting. I'm an idiot okay? No two ways about it. I didn't think where I was. Whose home I was shouting and swearing in. Let me go and I'll never come back. Never ever. Word of honor."

Then I'm explaining about the letter. How it was written, signed, and sent by a complete and total stranger. By nobody I'd ever met. Probably a trainee. A temp. How blind crazy mad I was the day it arrived. How furious I'd been, day and night, ever since. Edgy. Touchy. Sore. Quick to curse or quarrel at the drop of a hat. At nothing at all. Then telling about all the driving. Driving thousands of miles or more a week for decades. Driving in every kind of rotten weather. Weather so cold sometimes, snow piled so high it could have killed me, frozen me solid if my car broke down in the wrong place, too far out from people or towns.

Demon red eyes, unblinking still. I make a final plea. Bone cold. Played out. Desperate. "I'm leaving, okay? Turning around and swimming back to shore. I'm sorry. Really, really sorry. I meant no harm to you and yours. Just let me go and I'll never come back. But don't trick me okay? Please don't let me start swimming, thinking I'm safe, then shoot up from the depths and drill a hole through my soft, white belly, scatter my guts all around. Please don't do that."

Case made, I close my eyes and await the verdict. One, two, three seconds. I can't stand it. I open my eyes. Nothing there. Nothing at all. No disturbance on the surface of the water, not a ripple. Just gone. Vanished without a trace. Trick? Truce?

Frog swimming now, easy and slow, head up out of the water, making no sudden movements, I keep right on talking, hedging my bets. "When I get to shore, if you let me get to shore, I'll change my ways. Guaranteed. First thing I do, I apologize to my wife and my two grown sons. Apologize for being a fool and a hot head, just like my Old Man before me. Second thing I do, when I get back home, I get rid of every last reminder. Every vestige. The cheap suits and ties. The fray collar, button down shirts. The thick sole, rubber sole, orthopedic man shoes. And the belts. All those cracked, dime store belts." I kept on like that all the way back to shore.

Night School Confidential

Who was I to squawk? I'd quit teaching years back, but I had heat, lights, food, and rent to cover, so why not? Here's the way it worked: if six people showed up and paid, the class was a go. Less than six, they cancelled, that was how the guy at the adult education office explained it. Classes were held in a defunct two room elementary school five miles out from town at the junction of four frozen cornfields and two macadam section roads. The other half of the faculty was Leroy Sunderson, a semiretired septic tank installer.

With all the little farm towns hooking up with city water and sewer, Leroy's business was in a bad way. Small Animal Taxidermy was Leroy's subject. "Might as well make a few extra bucks off my hobby," was how he explained it. Rabbits, skunks, squirrels were Leroy's specialty, things he could count on finding when he was driving out country roads to do his job. The man had, over time, developed his own technique, has own approach.

"Anybody can stuff a dead squirrel, put it on a little painted board, glue on some acorns, call it taxidermy. Me, I got a gimmick. My stuff is unique. I use heavy-duty upholstery springs out of old chairs and sofas. I use top-of-the-line coat hangers. And, the secret of my success, I use a triggering device I designed myself. Like they use in rat traps, only more powerful. When it works right, people just go nuts. I tell them to look up close, see how lifelike the thing is there in the little painted habitat I made for it. They get up close, I yank the string, the trigger goes off, and bingo, the squirrel goes right for their throat. Great for all kinds of parties, a real icebreaker. Must have sold fifteen, twenty, to bars alone."

I had just quit one bad job, had no money put by, and was getting pretty desperate. That's why I answered the ad for this teaching job.

On opening night we were both there pretty early. I shoveled off the walk while Leroy got the furnace going and turned on the lights. We did everything we could think of to make it look like a big crowd was expected: great, tall coffeemaker Leroy borrowed from a church, four kinds of store-bought cookies, lots of stacked up styrofoam cups and paper plates, napkins. First impressions, we agreed, could make or break us.

I got eight the first night and Leroy got ten. Everybody paid up. Nobody dropped out. We were, me and Leroy, a going concern. Tuesday and Thursday nights, January through March, seven to ten, weather permitting.

Volunteers to read were never a problem in my All About Me writing class. Big Stan, a squat fat bald guy, always wanted to go first, read us the next, hot-off-the-press installment of his adventures as a freelance freight hauler. His first reading was typical.

"Anybody here ever been tapped on the back by fifty thousand volts of busted loose electricity?" he asked, looking, rapid fire, from face to face. Accepting, with glee, his uniqueness in regard to this sort of experience, he continued with equal frenzy.

"Well then, listen up. Truck quit on me. So there I am, walking down the godawfullest stretch of nowhere macadam I ever care to be all alone on in a lightning storm. BOOM! Something big cuts loose right behind me. I go to turn my head, see what all the fuss is about. BOOM! Just that fast there's another explosion, only this time I don't have no time to wonder where it's comin from. Lit me up bright blue like a neon sign and melted two, three inches of good India rubber off the soles of my shoes. Got the shoes to prove it too. Miracle I wasn't killed on the spot. Lightning bolt hit the power line, that's the first explosion. Power line hopped over and zapped me, that's the second one. Took enough juice through my body to kill ten full-grown mules and then some."

Pausing to fix each of us, one by one, with a squint eyed stare, he continued. "Lost ever hair I ever had." Pausing again with the slow grin that always preceded his finale. "Every hair up north," he rolled his eyes skyward, "and every bit of hair down south." He glanced, with a wink and a leer, at his crotch.

My classroom was small hot and airless. Everyone wore wool. Wool pants, shirts, coats, socks, and caps. Wool arrives, when damp, with a pungent memory of where it's been and shares that past, when heated, freely. Fried meat, burnt onions, wood smoke, cigarette smoke, gasoline, kerosene, and spilled beer were constant visitors to my class.

R. Jean, a no-nonsense reader, favored head to toe red and black check hunting outfits of heavy, unwashed wool. She read with no inflection and she read fast. Her other stylistic quirk, as reader and writer, was the repetition of a single blunt phrase.

"Okay, so I'm twelve, boyfriend, pregnant. I wasn't gonna marry him, NO WAY. Took off running. That was in Alabama. Slept any place I could find, fields, ditches, abandoned houses. Got to California. Had the baby. Social work people said I couldn't keep him, said they were gonna put him up for adoption. I told em they weren't gonna get no baby of mine without a fight, NO WAY. So, we're on the road again. Lived with a family in a blue Chevy station wagon a couple of months. Wound up in Detroit. Worked the shops around there and lived with a guy ten, twelve, years. One day he says my kid eats too much, says he makes too much racket. Says either my kid goes or he goes. I told him he wasn't gonna throw no kid of mine out without a fight, NO WAY. So, we're on the road again. Wound up in Flint. Worked the shops around there two, three, years. One day me and my boy are walkin by the boot factory. We're goin out to dinner. My boy holds his nose. Asks how come we all the time have to live in places that smell like rotten eggs. I told him we don't gotta live no place we don't want to, NO WAY. So we come here. I drive truck. I like car trips and parties where everyone brings some different kind of food."

When Vern read, we all got quiet, asked no questions, looked in any direction but his. "I think all the time. Can't stop thinking. I even think when I'm talking. Sometimes my wife gets mad because I think so much. But when she says how come I don't got word one for her anymore, and I tell her what I'm all the time thinking about, she gets mad.

So what do you do? If I think a thing I think it, nothing I can do about that. If somebody asks me what I got on my mind, and I tell 'em, and they get mad, nothing I can do about that either.

"Women. Okay, so a guy is working in a shop. He has a wife and a kid. Maybe he has two or three kids. He has a house or maybe a trailer. He has a car. He has these things he is paying on. If he stops paying on these things, he loses them. Loses his house or his trailer. Loses his car that he needs to get to work. He does not lose his wife and kids. So he gets laid off and a woman gets hired on. Who is gonna pay that man's bills? Who is gonna give that man's wife and kids a place to live, food to eat, and clothes to wear? Nobody. That is who. So why did they take and let him go? Women taking paychecks from men is wrong. Period. End of story."

If Vern made us all look away, Chuck made our skin crawl. His subject never changed.

"Okay, okay, okay, so you want to hear about dyin'? I'll tell you about dyin'. Up there you're watchin', all the time watchin' for any little thing, for Charlie. When it comes, it comes fast. You got no time to think. You got no time to ask questions. You got no time for nothing but to pump as many bullets as fast as you can into whatever it is. Charlie is down there waiting for you. Every helicopter gunner in 'Nam knows this. Charlie is always hiding down there in the jungle waiting for you. And Charlie is a little flame. He is a tiny little flame. If somebody don't put that flame out it'll spread and it will burn the whole world down to nothing but cinder and ashes. When I saw that I could stop that flame, saw that I could put that flame out if I pumped enough bullets into it, I knew I was alive. I knew the Lord Jesus sent me to that place to do his work. That was in 'Nam. I was on a destructive trip. Now, I'm on a creative trip. I want to be an actor in the movies. Maybe a musician or a painter. Something creative. And I know why that is, too."

Often, after he read, Chuck would get up and drift out of the classroom, out of the building, and stay away for an hour or more. He never said why he was going, and I never asked.

Lorraine was the last to read on the last night of class. Up until then she'd read papers about gardening, her cat, and her two hobbies:

collecting dishes that looked like nesting hens, where the bottom part was the nest and the top part the hen, and collecting birds' eggs. She hollowed out and arranged them by color and size on beds of cotton stuffing.

"My husband died," she began, almost in a whisper. "We'd only been married for three years, and he died of cancer. I didn't know what to do. Nothing made any sense if somebody as young and full of life as Larry could die like that. I quit going to church. I stopped seeing people. All I wanted to do was stay in the apartment where Larry and I had lived together, stay there and think things through. But after awhile I needed money. So I went to work delivering mail for the post office. They said it would be lonely work, driving out all the section roads to get letters and packages to all the farms in the middle of nowhere. I told them I didn't mind, that I'd be glad for the work, so they hired me."

Coughing, shifting around on chairs, rattling keys and coins, there were always a few background noises when somebody was reading their paper in class. For Lorraine, just then, it was pin drop quiet.

"I hadn't really talked to anybody for over a year. At least not the way you talk to a person when you try to listen for what they're really saying. I was like a sleepwalker, eating, working, doing laundry, but not really alive.

"So when the old man asked me a question, it surprised me. I wasn't expecting it. He lived out in the country in a tiny farmhouse all drifted around with snow. I had a package he had to sign for. Special delivery. He answered the door. His skin was light blue, like maybe he'd painted himself up for a party or a joke."

"He said he wanted to ask me something. I was halfway back to my truck when I heard him call out. Heard him ask me to come back up on the porch for a minute, that he had something to ask me.

"His voice was hard to hear. I had to lean in close to make out what he was saying. He said he was a lonely old man with a blue face. That the medicine I'd just delivered made his skin blue. He had to take the medicine, but it made his skin blue.

"Then he asked me if I would kiss him. Kiss him on the cheek and make him feel better. I got embarrassed and I didn't know what to do, but I kissed him on the cheek, shook his hand, and then drove away. I've never told this story to anybody before. Never once."

For a long time nobody spoke. Then Big Stan shouted out that he once had to take a pill that made him piss blue, but he'd never heard of a pill that made your skin blue.

When we finished up that night, Leroy gave me a stuffed, spring-loaded squirrel with its paws up around its ears like maybe it was tearing its hair out. "Icebreaker," said the note, tied to a tiny paw with twine. "Hundred percent guaranteed."

Goodbyes said, everybody drifted off and they were long gone by the time I finally left the building. Outside in the dark, with all the lights of the school off, I stood listening, looking around. There were more stars in the sky than I could remember ever seeing. I heard sounds, clear and separate: somebody talking somewhere, a dog yipping like it was tethered and straining to get loose. Sounds amplified well beyond their normal range, then gone, abruptly, in the resonant stillness of a land under snow.

ACKNOWLEDGMENTS

The stories "I Get This Telegram," "Instant Gandhi," "I'll See You in Jail," "Religious Instruction," "Time's Up," and "I'm Not From Around Here" first appeared, in slightly different form, under the title "Instant Gandhi," in *War, Literature & the Arts*. The story "Night School Confidential," also in a slightly different form, first appeared in *Harvard Review*. The story "Dime Store Belts" first appeared in the online literary magazine, *The Periphery*. "Rubber on Wheels" appeared in *The Coachella Review*. "Roughcut" first appeared in *Harvard Review Online*. Special thanks to Dr. Jerry Yee, M.D. for invaluable help with manuscript preparation.

CPSIA information can be obtained
at www.ICGtesting.com
Printed in the USA
FFHW02n1206230818
48007285-51701FF

9 781680 031652